CW00455919

Praise for the Lila Maclean Academic Mystery Series

"A pitch-perfect portrayal of academic life with a beguiling cast of anxious newbies, tweedy old troublemakers and scholars as sharp as they're wise. Lila's Stonedale is a world I'm thrilled to have found. Roll on book two!"

– Catriona McPherson,
Multi-Award-Winning Author of the Dandy Gilver Series

"Takes the reader into higher education's secrets and shadows, where the real lesson is for the new professor—how to stay alive. If you're smart, you'll read this book."

– Lori Rader-Day,
Anthony Award-Winning Author of *The Black Hour*

"Entertaining, intricate, and oh-so-smart! The talented Cynthia Kuhn treats mystery lovers to an insider's look at the treacherous world of academia—seething with manipulation, jealousy, and relentless ambition. A terrific plot."

— Hank Phillippi Ryan,
Mary Higgins Clark Award-Winning Author

"A very intricate, cool story featuring the depth of an institution where everyone is dying to climb the ladder of success."

– *Suspense Magazine*

"Tightly plotted with a deliciously memorable cast of characters, *The Art of Vanishing* kept me guessing from start to finish, and Kuhn's smart sense of humor made every page a pleasure."

– Marla Cooper,
Author of the Kelsey McKenna Destination Wedding Mysteries

"Absolutely addictive."

— Kathleen Valenti,
Agatha-Nominated Author of the Maggie O'Malley Mysteries

"Whether Stonedale University English professor Lila is confronting a backstabbing colleague or investigating a murder attempt on a cantankerous bestselling author, readers will root for this enormously likeable heroine."

— Ellen Byron,
USA Today Bestselling Author of *Plantation Shudders*

"Smart, action-packed, and immensely satisfying, *The Subject of Malice* had me from page one. I love this series, and it just keeps getting better."

– Wendy Tyson,
Author of *Ripe for Vengeance*

"A pure delight from page one. Cynthia Kuhn's Lila Maclean mysteries will cure what ails you. Funny and fantastic."

— Becky Clark,
Author of the Mystery Writer's Mysteries

"A twisty mystery with a gentle, gracious humor and a touch of whimsy. Reading it is like spending the afternoon with a best friend. You laugh. You smile. And you want to see her again very soon. I can't wait for the next Lila Maclean mystery."

— Keenan Powell,
Agatha-Nominated Author of the Maeve Malloy Mystery Series

"Papers, and panels, and murder, oh my! Everyone's favorite professor, Lila Maclean (secret powers include reading and finding bodies), is back and she's on the case (officially)! Lila's latest adventure is full of high drama and high crimes. Such FUN!"

— Julie Mulhern,
USA Today Bestselling Author of the Country Club Murders

"An intelligent, witty mystery that will keep you guessing to the very end."

— Libby Klein,
Author of the Poppy McAllister Mysteries

THE STUDY OF SECRETS

The Lila Maclean Academic Mystery Series
by Cynthia Kuhn

THE SEMESTER OF OUR DISCONTENT (#1)
THE ART OF VANISHING (#2)
THE SPIRIT IN QUESTION (#3)
THE SUBJECT OF MALICE (#4)
THE STUDY OF SECRETS (#5)

THE STUDY OF SECRETS

A Lila Maclean Academic Mystery

Cynthia Kuhn

HENERY PRESS

Copyright

THE STUDY OF SECRETS
A Lila Maclean Academic Mystery
Part of the Henery Press Mystery Collection

First Edition | May 2020

Henery Press, LLC
www.henerypress.com

Author photograph by Angela Kleinsasser

Trade Paperback ISBN-13: 978-1-63511-615-1
Digital epub ISBN-13: 978-1-63511-616-8
Kindle ISBN-13: 978-1-63511-617-5
Hardcover ISBN-13: 978-1-63511-618-2

Printed in the United States of America

For my family (near and far)

ACKNOWLEDGMENTS

Henery Press—for your terrific work on this series.

The Hen House, Sisters in Crime (National, Guppies, and Colorado chapters), Mystery Writers of America (National and RMMWA), International Thriller Writers, Malice Domestic, Left Coast Crime, Short Mystery Fiction Society, House of Clues, and MSU Denver—for the community and inspiration.

Mary Angela, Gretchen Archer, Jim Aubrey, Mark Baker, Margarita Barceló, Francelia Belton, Mary Birk, Micki Browning, Lori Caswell, Wendy and Seth Crichton, Annette Dashofy, E.B. Davis, Sandra Doe, Amy Drayer, Dru Ann, Claire Fishback, Debra Goldstein, Dorothy and William Guerrera, Elsie Haley, Elena Hartwell, Sybil Johnson, Jennifer Kincheloe, Libby Klein, Dennis and Ursula Kuhn, Kate Lansing, Catriona McPherson, Margaret Mizushima, Julie Mulhern, Sandra Murphy, Barbara Nickless, Nora Page, Vincent Piturro, Keenan Powell, Christy and Bob Rowe, Renée Ruderman, Harriette Sackler, Angela Sanders, Meredith Schorr, Nancy Cole Silverman, Craig Svonkin, Wendy Tyson, Susan Van Kirk, LynDee Walker, Wendolyn Weber, Kristopher Zgorski, and the entire SinC-CO book club—for generous words and/or encouragement.

Ann Perramond—for being such a brilliant and inspiring critique partner; Jane Brucklacher—for excellent proofreading; and Dorothy Guerrera—for providing essential commentary and delightful asides.

The fabulous Chicks on the Case—Ellen Byron, Becky Clark, Marla Cooper, Vickie Fee, Kellye Garrett, Leslie Karst, Lisa Q. Mathews, and Kathleen Valenti—for everything blog, book, and way beyond.

Amazing family (Guerreras, Crichtons, Kuhns, Peterkas, West-Repperts, Hundertmarks, Abneys, and Welshes), friends, and readers—for your support. It means the world.

My dearest Mom, Dad, and Wen—for your kindness and laughter, since forever.

My beloved Kenneth, Griffin, and Sawyer—for your epic patience, sweetness, humor, and sunshine.

Endless gratitude and love.

Chapter 1

"Have you found any buried treasure in the study?" Bibi asked, pouring me another cup of tea. I pretended to consider this. How could I admit outright that there was not a single item I didn't find fascinating? I had examined every page, list, scrap, and scribble I'd come across. Even her jar of paper clips seemed meaningful.

I didn't usually pay that much attention to people's desks, but when you are allowed to rifle through the study of your favorite writer, it's almost as though you've been granted a glimpse into the other side of a magical spell. Here is where they created the world into which you have immersed. Here is where they developed the characters you love and sent them on their journeys. Here is where they put word after word onto the page, through sheer will and imagination. Here is where the author Isabella Dare lived.

I'd met Isabella, whose married name was Bibi Callahan, at the Malice in the Mountains literary conference we'd attended last spring. It had been one of the greatest shocks of my life, recognizing that the woman standing before me was the author of the books I'd devoted my life to studying over the past decade. Then I realized that she'd heard me talking about her books all weekend at the conference. Before I knew who she was, I'd even held forth on the subject for quite some time while the two of us waited in line to get coffee after a panel.

Still blushed every time I remembered that.

But she had been intrigued by what she'd heard, and at the end of the conference, she'd offered me the use of her guest cottage during my sabbatical from Stonedale University. In return, I had agreed to organize her study at Callahan House, which was a Victorian Painted Lady—in shades of ruby, amethyst, emerald, and citrine—with towers, gables, carved bands, decorative shingles, and other delightful ornamentation. It was famous as the first home built in Larkston, Colorado by silver mining magnate Godfrey Callahan. The previous generations of Callahans had sold off parts of their land to create the college that bore their name and to the town of Larkston as it grew but retained a large swath of forest around the mansion and Silver Rush Lake behind it to preserve privacy. I'd heard bits and pieces of the history from Bibi, who had married into the Callahan family. As the only remaining member, she had inherited the responsibility of taking care of the site. Visitors were drawn to the whimsical style and priceless antiques; tours were allowed to parade through the home by appointment. She graciously allowed access to everything except for any occupied bedrooms and the study, which were cordoned off with velvet ropes on such days.

Currently, she was perched on the window seat in the library, where we ate our lunches. I was on the other side of the small wooden table with a view of the long driveway that meandered gracefully through the snowy pine trees toward the house. We were surrounded by floor-to-ceiling bookshelves. Most of them were filled with mysteries, including the Isabella Dare books, which were modestly tucked in among the others rather than displayed prominently. Additional shelves held intriguing items from Bibi's world travels, and a splendid painting of moonlight on the nearby lake hung above the fireplace. The black curved leather sofa and club chairs were worn to perfection and arranged around an oversized round ottoman. It was an altogether welcoming room.

The grandfather clock in the hallway—large enough for us to climb into if we had the notion—chimed softly. Bibi set down her teacup and smoothed her white braid. She was wearing a thick maroon cardigan over a long black dress. The sweater was a homemade concoction with some lumps and gaps. She'd taken up knitting after her retirement from teaching English and frequently commented on her lack of mastery, but I thought her pieces were downright artistic.

"Everything in the study is interesting," I admitted finally.

She laughed. "I find that very hard to believe."

"It is," I insisted. Although officially I'd spent much of the fall revising the book on which my tenure bid next year would hang, which was a study of Isabella Dare's mysteries, I was also trying my hand at a mystery novel—a secret I'd shared only with a select few. Thus, being in the study was inspiring in more ways than one.

The lines around her vivid green eyes creased pleasantly when she smiled. "I still plan to stay out of the way until you have organized it completely—nothing worse than someone *hovering* over you as you try to make headway on a project, is there?—but I do confess that I'm curious as to what you're finding. My method is to scurry into the room, put the paperwork on top of any available pile, then scuttle out again. When I retired from Callahan College, I dumped the papers in there without even a smidgen of organizational purpose. As you can see."

"No worries," I assured her. "I've already sorted everything into folders. Do you have any thoughts on the order in which you want things filed?"

"Oh no," she said, clearly horrified. "I detest sorting things. Just file them however you see fit. Or shove them into the cabinets willy nilly. I'll adapt to whatever you come up with. As long as they're out of sight, I'll be ecstatic, thank you. I can't tell you how grateful I am for your help."

I nodded. "It's the least I could do. Thank you so much for letting me stay here."

"It's been a pleasure."

I pushed away the thought that in mid-January—just one short month—spring term would begin. I was already becoming somewhat despondent at the thought of having to leave this little scholarly utopia. At least the holidays were in between, as a buffer.

"I'm anxious about tonight—" she began, then shook her head slightly. "Scratch that. I'm *more* anxious about getting some writing done this afternoon, so let's get back to work."

Bibi didn't like to talk about her books while they were in progress, I'd learned. I didn't know what this one was about or how far along she was. All I knew was that she wrote at different locations throughout the mansion. Once she'd told me that the regular change of scenery was a valuable part of her creative process. And in this place, she had plenty of rooms to choose from.

The first floor had a stunning foyer with a wrought-iron-and-crystal chandelier. On the left was a parlor, kitchen, and dining room; on the right was a library, powder room, and study. In the center was a great room so large it echoed. All of the rooms had been painted in jewel tone colors and furnished primarily with heirlooms. The bedrooms upstairs were as exquisite as the rooms on the first floor. Two of them were round, like the parlor and library below; the towers were by far my favorite element of the house.

I followed Bibi into the kitchen, where we quickly cleaned the lunch dishes, then began gathering items together for this evening's book club meeting. She had asked me to lead the conversation, which I had agreed to do as long as we read the first Isabella Dare book. Bibi had reluctantly acquiesced, though I suspected now that the day had arrived, she was having second thoughts. I was confident that afterwards, she would be glad we'd done it.

"I have to tell you something before everyone arrives," Bibi said, handing me a stack of yellow plates.

I set them on the granite island. "What is it?"

"You weren't planning on me saying anything, right? I mean, about who I am." She rolled her hand toward me. "As an author."

"Your friends don't know that you're Isabella Dare?"

Bibi extracted water glasses from a cabinet and passed them to me, one by one. "They never knew me by that name. My sister Ilse couldn't pronounce Isabella, so she called me Bibi, which stuck. When my father passed away and our mother remarried, we took my stepfather's last name. Then we moved from New York to Larkston, my mother enrolled us in elementary school as Ilse and Bibi Smithson, and that was who we were from that point on. My stepfather didn't last long as a member of the family, but his name persisted."

I admired the delicate etched daisies on the glasses as I put them with the plates. "I see. And you don't want anyone to know that you're a mystery writer?"

"It was all so long ago. We could discuss the book as if it were written by someone else, couldn't we?" Bibi retrieved two oval platters with a sunflower pattern from a nearby shelf, then went back for matching serving bowls.

"We could." I didn't want to pressure her, though I believed the book club members would be overjoyed to realize that the author was their friend. "Did anyone know about the books?"

"My grandparents—on my mother's side—did. I lived with them in New York while I went to graduate school, and the books were published during that time." She smiled wryly as she removed white cloth napkins from a drawer and placed them next to the platters. "I never imagined that I'd end up back at Callahan College, but after I married Jamie, who proposed at graduation, the family encouraged the English department to make a place for me."

"And you were happy there?"

"Oh, yes. But prior to that happening, I worried that having written popular fiction might count against me as a candidate for any literature position, that schools wouldn't take me seriously. It was different in those days..." she paused. "Or maybe it wasn't. Anyway, you know what I mean."

Oh yes, I knew. During my first conversation with Roland Higgins, the then-chair of our department, he had gone apoplectic when I'd asked if I could teach a mystery course. He'd taken the opportunity to lecture me on what counted as literature and what didn't.

In his opinion.

Which differed greatly from my own.

Bibi emerged from the pantry with two vases. "So for the novels, I used a name that both was and was not mine at the same time. It was somehow easier to think of Isabella Dare as the writer and Bibi Callahan as the academic. If the books had become bestsellers, I would have told everyone in the universe that I wrote them. But they didn't even make a ripple. It was a small publisher who went under soon afterwards, and that seemed to be that. I swore my grandparents to secrecy and as far as I know, they kept my secret until the end. Gradually, the books came to seem like something I'd done in another lifetime." After rummaging around in a drawer, she held up a green tablecloth and shook it triumphantly. "Aha!"

"What about Jamie?"

"He knew everything, of course, but the rest of the Callahans didn't know my original name, so they didn't make the connection. I never saw fit to tell them."

It was the first time she'd talked this much about her personal life other than to say that her husband had passed away, I realized with a start. All of our conversations had been neatly steered toward books.

"You didn't tell your sister or mother?"

"I did not," she said, in a tone that put an end to that line of questioning.

I swerved. "Is Ilse your only sibling?"

"Yes." Her eyes, usually so bright, seemed to dim. She surveyed the items on the island. "Let's set up the rest of this later. The day's getting away from us, and I am desperate to get back to work."

"How's your book going?"

"It's a mystifying snarl of uncertain potential, as usual."

When Bibi left, I returned to the study. Unlike the other rooms in the house, which were tidy and sunny, the study was dark, with murky gray wallpaper, a black damask carpet, and heavy curtains on the arched windows made of material so thick that they only opened about a third of the way. The sunlight didn't have much of a chance to penetrate the gloom.

When I'd first gone into the room months ago, the task ahead of me was daunting. I'd had to deconstruct mountains of paper, arrange everything by topic, then whittle the material down even more into specific folders. The majority of items were from her professorial life and informative in their own way. Yet it was a thrill to come across papers relating to her novels, such as correspondence with her editor and publisher as well as manuscripts, notes, and galleys. Those discoveries were invaluable for developing my book focused on her fiction, which I hoped would eventually help promote her mysteries to a wider audience.

Glad to have arrived at the end of the endeavor, I began slipping the folders, in alphabetical order, into the shiny new file cabinets that had been installed below the long row of windows.

Previously, Bibi had used the built-in bookshelves on the opposite side to stack papers since there was a separate library, but now that they were empty, she planned to fill them with art pieces. She also intended to update the wallpaper and curtains, lighten up the color scheme. Before long, this study would be transformed.

Hours later, after I'd filed the last folder, I stood and surveyed the room. It was clean. Sighing happily, I bent forward and reached toward the floor to stretch my back. As I bobbed gently, a glint of something caught my eye. I moved over and knelt down by the vintage mahogany desk by the back window. It was facing away from the view of the large lake surrounded by pines. If this was my office, the first thing I'd do would be to turn it around, give myself something to look at while I worked. But perhaps Bibi found it to be too much of a distraction.

I peered underneath the desk, using the flashlight from my phone to cut through the shadows, and discovered a long silver key with an elaborately scrolled design on the top. It looked old both in style and patina. I crawled around the desk and saw a lock on the bottom drawer. Holding my breath, I inserted the key, which turned smoothly. The drawer rolled out noiselessly to reveal a thick stack of papers.

I paused and tapped my finger on the chair. Should I peek? I didn't want to intrude on anything private.

Then again, Bibi hadn't told me that anything was off limits, and she'd been very clear about the fact that the entire study needed to be organized.

I reached down into the drawer and removed the stack. The first sheet was blank, but the second was typewritten.

THE SECRETS OF EVERWELL

By Isabella Dare

I caught my breath. Was this an Athena Bolt mystery? The title structure followed that of the other three books, and she'd used the Dare form of her name.

I knew it wasn't the book she was working on right now—she had mentioned that her current practice was not to print anything out until the first full draft was completed. Otherwise, she said, the pages would "tempt her to fiddle with it too much."

In addition, these pages were typed, not printed. I ran my finger lightly over the title, feeling the almost imperceptible dents in the paper. Had this been written at the same time as the other books in the series? Was it unpublished?

If so, this manuscript, my scholarly self whispered excitedly, could be a major find.

I was turning carefully to the second page when my phone pinged with a text from Bibi. *Do you need any help getting ready for tonight?*

A quick glance at my watch showed that it was only hours from the gathering, and I needed to run to the store for food. With a great deal of regret, I put the manuscript carefully back into the drawer and pocketed the key.

It would have to wait.

Chapter 2

At eight thirty, after the guests had some time to eat, chat, and make themselves comfortable, book club was underway. I hadn't had a chance to talk to Bibi—between setting up the food and arranging flowers, there wasn't a minute to spare. I had barely managed to take a quick shower, dress in a long black jacket over jeans, and braid my dark wavy hair before the first person arrived. But now we were all in the parlor, everyone had partaken of the refreshments, and it was showtime.

Bibi invited our guests to take a seat. The Callahans had selected a sapphire palette for this room and filled it with sofas and chairs that had intricately carved wooden frames and rested on slender feet. The curves and scrolls reminded me of the key that was in my pocket. I couldn't wait to ask about the manuscript after the women left. Once everyone had selected a spot, Bibi welcomed them. She'd traded her lumpy cardigan for a sleek silver duster and added a chunky necklace that shimmered in the lamplight. "We are in for a real treat. Dr. Maclean here wrote the first dissertation ever focused on the work of Isabella Dare. She has spent years turning that study into a book. The depth and breadth of research she has performed makes her—and I'm not exaggerating here—the world's foremost authority on the subject."

"Oh," I said, startled. "I wouldn't say—"

"Oh *yes*. She is," Bibi said, then turned to me. "You are, Lila."

The guests applauded.

I greeted the group. The Larks, as they referred to themselves, had become friends in elementary school and remained close into their sixties: Margot Van Brewer worked with the administration at Callahan College; Penelope Salton was one of Bibi's former English department colleagues; and Gillian Shane had recently retired from her own literary agency. Having met Bibi's friends at one time or another over the past few months, I was looking forward to hearing what they thought about the book.

The four women spent a great deal of time together and had that sort of easy sparkle that long-term friendships can possess. They were all strong, smart women who genuinely cared about one another, and they knew how to have a good time. The occasional dinners in which they'd included me had been full of laughter. They had married their high-school boyfriends: Winston Van Brewer, Brody Salton, Hudson Shane, and Jamie Callahan. The latter two men were no longer alive, having been in a car accident years earlier; the group had not only supported each other through that terrible time but also continued to honor their friends with frequent allusions to fond memories.

"Thank you for those kind words and for hosting us, Bibi." I picked up my precious copy of *The Case of the Wandering Spirit.* Out of nowhere, I found myself having to blink back tears at the sight of multiple people holding the book I loved. Because it was an older, out-of-print book from a defunct press, it had taken effort to gather enough copies for all of us to read the novel at once. Thanks to the power of the internet, I'd been able to make that happen. But outside of my dissertation committee, this was the first discussion with a group of others who had read an Isabella Dare book. It was my secret goal to convince a university press to reprint the series, possibly in a scholarly edition that included contextual materials and essays in the back so that many others could read, teach, and enjoy the books. But this evening was a milestone in its own way. I could have wept with joy.

Summoning my most professional demeanor, I cleared my throat. "Thank you all for coming. If you have a question or thought as we go along, please feel free to share. Shall we begin with initial impressions?"

"Do you mean whether we liked it or not?" Gillian asked, with a nod that set her brown corkscrew curls bouncing. They were collected by a clasp at the back of her neck but sprang out in every direction. Although she was retired, she still dressed as if she were about to attend an important meeting at any minute, favoring tailored suits, scarves, and heels. She reached into the briefcase next to her chair and pulled out an expensive pen and leather-bound notepad.

I tried again. "Perhaps a list of the issues it raised for you?"

"Goodness, we don't usually do *that*," Margot said with a throaty laugh and shake of her impossibly red bob. Even if you didn't know anything about her, you would have guessed that she was once a fashion model. Slim, chic, and seemingly flawless, Margot was perched on the sofa next to Bibi, her back as straight as a board. There was something feline about her features, perhaps a result of whatever plastic surgery magic had erased any hint of wrinkles. She turned her hazel eyes toward me. "Right away, we go around the room and say whether we loved or hated it."

"Yes, and it's always one or the other, Lila. We never seem to feel in the middle about anything," Penelope said, from a chair near the fireplace. Her large brown eyes, freckles, and often tentative manner had more than once brought to mind a fawn surprised in the woods. She brushed back her faded blonde shoulder-length hair and smiled. "I know there are other discussions to be had, but we do have our traditions."

"Let's start there, then."

"You first, Lila?" Penelope asked faintly.

"Sure. From the beginning, I knew *The Case of the Wandering Spirit* was extraordinary. It makes use of genre conventions in a way that both affirms and challenges them. Dare's ability to create and sustain suspense while tending to the complexities of character is absolutely superb."

Bibi coughed.

"Moreover, the author incorporates social critique in an engaging but not preachy manner, which is a difficult feat indeed. Tonight, I hope we'll be able to dig into why the story works on so many levels."

"Good idea," Margot said. "I'm game to go along with this format as long as we get to say if we liked the book. That's my favorite part."

"Before we go any further, I'll mention that there are other books in the Athena Bolt series: *The Case of the Wandering Spirit*, *The Raven at the Door*, and *The Whisper in the Wall.* All are fantastic."

"There are more books after this?" Penelope applauded. "I can't wait to read them."

"They may be hard to find," I said. "But they're well worth the effort."

I didn't mention that Bibi had a copy of each one on her library shelves; she could offer them if she had a mind to do so.

One by one, they shared their thoughts about the book. Everyone except Bibi—no one appeared to notice that she hadn't given an opinion—said they had loved it, and I wasn't surprised. Whenever someone asked me to describe Isabella Dare's writing, I said it was like Agatha Christie meets Shirley Jackson with a twist. When I brought that up and asked if it was a fair description, the group agreed. We talked about the many Gothic elements, the structure of the mystery, the subversive aspects, and Dare's masterful creation of suspense.

Margot fluttered an elegant hand. "What else do you know about Isabella Dare?"

It was exceedingly difficult not to make eye contact with Bibi.

I looked down at the book and tried to explain without lying. "The author biography you have on the back cover here, the one that says she 'lived a quiet life in New York City' is in fact about as much as *can* be said about her." Hearing that tortured sentence emerge prompted me to keep talking in an effort to erase the memory of it as quickly as possible. "The first book came out in the late 1970s, but the press was long gone by the time I found her books, so I couldn't ask them directly. I reached out to various agents and other publishers in an attempt to rummage up information, but that didn't go anywhere, either. I also have performed internet searches at various intervals over the years and there's nothing out there."

"But—" Margot began.

"At all," I said, firmly. "Nothing."

"So you don't have direct information from the author in your own book, then?" Gillian looked up from her notetaking, confused. "Nothing authoritative?"

My mind raced. Although it's not necessary to interview an author for a critical study, I had indeed done so. And Gillian had raised an issue that I hadn't yet considered: I'd incorporated the author interviews into the revised version of my book that I was planning to submit to a university press. There was no way I could keep the fact that I'd met with Isabella Dare a secret if I quoted them, but we'd never talked about how to handle it if people started asking questions about her current whereabouts.

An even more chilling thought descended: if she didn't agree to exist, so to speak, I wouldn't be able to use her words as support for my claims in the first place.

"Well..." I drew out the word as long as I could without knowing what I was going to say next.

Bibi's eyes met mine. After a long moment, she sighed, rose from the sofa, went to the fireplace, and faced the group. "Okay then. Buckle up, Larks. I will tell you something that cannot leave this room. Invoking the shroud of secrecy. No one hears what I'm about to tell you, including your husbands. Agreed?"

Each woman silently patted her heart two times, which was something I'd observed them doing before whenever the Larks made a promise. Assured of their pledge, Bibi continued. "*I* am Isabella Dare."

The room went silent.

Then Margot threw back her head and laughed. "Good one, Bibi."

"It's true," I said. "She is."

There were gasps, and the three women exchanged glances, as if checking for consensus on how to respond.

Eventually, Margot rolled her eyes. "How about start at the beginning, please?"

Bibi recounted everything she'd told me earlier about why she'd written the series under the Dare name. By the end, the Larks were staring at her, open-mouthed.

Margot took a long drink, then set down her glass. "So your whole life, you kept that a secret from us, your *best friends*?"

"I didn't know how to tell you," Bibi said. "But the books went out of print and I didn't write any more novels. As time went on, it seemed less and less important. I'm sorry."

"We could have been working together this whole time!" Gillian exclaimed, tossing one end of her cheery yellow scarf over her shoulder. "I could have done so much for you."

Bibi blew her a kiss. "I appreciate that, dear friend."

"Sorry, I'm still processing. You wrote *three* mysteries?"

Penelope asked, in a tone of disbelief.

"Four," I heard myself say.

Bibi twisted her head toward me. "What do you mean?"

"Never mind. It was nothing." I hoped she would leave it at that.

Instead, she repeated the question.

The silence in the room pressed in until I couldn't stand it anymore. "Didn't you write *four* mysteries?"

Bibi blinked. "Why do you think that?"

"I found a manuscript in the study."

She looked blank. "In the study? I don't know what you're talking about. What was the title?"

I hesitated, but her focus was intense, and I couldn't see a way out of it. "Ever-something."

Bibi gasped. "*The Secrets of Everwell*?"

The reactions were even louder this time, and someone emitted a little scream. The color drained from Bibi's face. When she started to sway, I jumped up and helped her back to the sofa, where her friends surrounded her, delegating tasks to each other. Soon she was propped up with pillows and people were fanning her.

I went into the kitchen and ran cool water over a towel.

Gillian bustled in a moment later and put the kettle on. "Lila, what can you tell me about the manuscript?"

"I didn't read it. It was in a locked drawer in the study."

She raised an eyebrow. "Locked?"

"Yes. Oh! That reminds me..." I removed the silver key from my pocket and set it on the counter. "I need to return this to Bibi."

Gillian picked it up and examined the design. "Pretty key. Someone could wear this as a necklace." She pulled out Bibi's favorite cup and saucer, the one decorated with violets, from the cabinet and set the key down next to them. "I'll give it to her. I'm bringing in this tea anyway."

"That's kind of you, but—"

"I *insist*." She paused and slipped the key into her own pocket before adding, "No offense, honey, but maybe you should give Bibi a little space right now."

Perhaps she was right. Gillian knew her far better than I ever would; if she believed Bibi was upset with me, I should listen.

And I didn't blame Bibi one bit. I'd certainly made a mess of things.

Margot floated in, asking if we needed any help. I gave her the damp towel for Bibi, and she floated out again.

I placed a spoon and napkin on the small silver tray that Bibi used to carry her tea around the mansion. "Gillian, you don't think anyone will say anything, do you? I feel awful for blurting out Bibi's secret."

She came around the island and took both of my hands. "Word's not going to get out. We've been close friends for decades—we're practically sisters—and we keep each other's secrets. Remember that she *chose* to tell us about herself because she trusts us. You didn't betray any confidences. There's not a safer place in the world where you could have mentioned the book. Don't worry."

Hearing the shrill whistle of the kettle, Gillian dropped my hands and snatched it up. She poured steaming water into the cup, looking thoughtful. "The fourth one hasn't been published yet, right?"

"I don't think so. It's in manuscript form, and I've never come across a book with that title in my research. But I haven't had a chance to clarify anything with Bibi yet, so I can't be certain." I sighed. "Now I'm almost afraid to bring it up again. Look how she responded at the mere mention of it."

"Too bad I'm retired," Gillian said, smiling ruefully. "And now I'm moving to the beach and planning to exist primarily on fruit slices and drinks with umbrellas in them. What perfectly awful timing that was."

I opened the drawer and handed her the box of Bibi's peppermint tea.

"I wonder if she has the rights for the first three," Gillian mused, as she removed a teabag and submerged it. "The one we read for today was fabulous, and I'm not just saying that because she's one of my oldest and most beloved friends. What are the others like?"

"They're wonderful."

"Maybe she should republish them all."

"My whole purpose in life has been to make that happen," I said. I told her about the scholarly editions that I'd already pitched to several university presses, hoping that they'd be able to secure the appropriate permissions from a representative for the previous publisher to reprint the mysteries. The idea had not, so far, gained any traction—primarily because no one knew who Isabella Dare was. My colleagues had advised me to focus instead on publishing the study of her work that I needed for my tenure bid, which would bring her to the attention of other literary critics, then return to my efforts to help the Isabella Dare mysteries themselves find a new audience.

Of course that was before I met the author in person. Now everything had changed. Although I'd been talking to Bibi about the idea, she'd been extremely reluctant. She wasn't convinced that anyone would want to read them in the first place—even though a real-life-Isabella-Dare-fan was sitting right in front of her.

"We should chat after the holidays," Gillian said, tapping her chin. "Between the two of us, we may be able to nudge her with a plan."

A flicker of excitement surged up. Perhaps Gillian could convince Bibi to republish the series and launch the newly discovered fourth book.

Though I had to wonder if Bibi's reaction meant she had no intention of publishing it.

Or of anyone seeing it, ever.

After Gillian left with the tea, I arranged some cookies on a plate and tidied up the kitchen, then returned to the parlor. Winston and Brody, who had been drinking scotch in the library—their activity of choice on book club nights, I'd been told—were now mingling with the other attendees. The women also had drinks in hand and the volume of conversation was increasing; it was as though the book club discussion had spontaneously transformed into a cocktail party.

I made my way through the group to Bibi, who was sitting upright on the sofa, sipping her tea. I set the cookies on the table. She picked one up and nibbled it.

"I'm so sorry, Bibi."

"It's fine, dear. *I'm* sorry that my reaction was slightly over the top." She waved the cookie around in a circle. "I'd completely forgotten about the book. Just saying the title out loud brought back a lot of memories that I'd left behind."

"I feel terrible."

"Oh, please don't. Not for an instant." Bibi took another small bite. "There was already a lot going on at that moment. I'd admitted to my friends that I'd never told them about my mysteries, which was surprisingly emotional. Cathartic, in a way, but nothing like I imagined it would be." She winced. "But now I do have a beast of a headache. Could you bring things to a close for me? The men came in to determine the cause of the hubbub, and well, you can see for yourself that it seems unlikely we'll be able to press on with our book club discussion. I would prefer some quiet if at all possible."

"Of course." I looked around, determining that Margot was the logical choice to put in charge of shutting things down. She had a way about her that was commanding but gracious.

Since she was on the far side of the parlor, near the hallway, I decided to double back and cut through the kitchen. There were fewer people to push through, as people were coming and going, replenishing their drinks.

As I moved through the kitchen, I heard a terrified shriek. I ran down the long main hallway toward the sound and turned the corner to see Penelope in the doorway of the study, trembling. One hand was clasped over her mouth; the other was pointing at something on the floor.

There was a motionless Gillian, her bright scarf twisted unforgivingly around her throat as she stared upwards, unblinking.

Chapter 3

I wished I were the kind of person who had never been on the scene of a crime, but I've had the misfortune to be around more than my share. So after I checked Gillian's pulse to confirm what I knew to be true—I was never sure if that counted as contaminating the scene, but it had to be done—I told Penelope to call 911 and not let anyone into the room. Then I ran to the parlor, where I told Bibi what had happened as quietly as I could, stressing that contrary to what we'd already discussed about wrapping things up, no one should leave the premises.

She leapt to her feet and raised her voice, explaining that a serious incident had taken place, prompting startled reactions. Then she cast me a look that I interpreted as her wanting me to take over from there.

"Please stay where you are, everyone. The police are on their way. It's extremely important that no one move." Although I meant *don't leave*, not *don't move,* everyone stood perfectly still, glancing around uneasily, perhaps also doing the math to determine who was not in the room. The wail of sirens cut into the silence, growing louder the longer that we all stared at each other. Bibi went to the front door and opened it. Several cars, gumballs flashing, were racing up the drive, their tires crunching against the snow.

I slipped down the hallway, to where Penelope was leaning against the wall, crying. "Who could have done this to her? Gillian is the *best.*"

I patted her on the shoulder and gave my own brimming eyes a swipe. "I'm so sorry."

Penelope straightened up and tugged her shirt down, though it didn't address any of the wrinkles. Tears streamed down her face.

"How did you happen to find her?" I asked.

She sniffed a few times. "Once we got Bibi squared away on the couch and you were in the kitchen, we were talking about the manuscript you'd mentioned. Then Bibi started saying that you had done marvels with her study, so when it became clear that she was fine, I went to have a quick peek." Penelope wiped her eyes. "Do you think I can leave now? I'd like to be with my husband."

"I think you'd better wait here—the police are going to want to talk to you, and they have pulled up out front. But I can find Brody and ask him to come back here, if you like."

She nodded dejectedly.

I was starting to feel like a ping pong ball, bouncing back and forth between rooms, but Penelope deserved support, so off I went, racing down the hallway and into the parlor, where I explained to her husband that he needed to come with me. His eyebrows shot up and he moved immediately forward. I led him to the study, aiming for the clump of police officers surrounding Penelope. We waited for a few minutes as they spoke with her, then she caught sight of Brody, and her face lit up.

A tall man in a blue suit said something to the officer standing next to him, who went into the study. I froze. From the back, the man bore a strong resemblance to Detective Lexington Archer, whom I had dated for several years. Same powerful build, same purposeful energy, same spiky dark hair. Once he turned around, the impression faded. He was attractive, but he wasn't Lex.

"And you are?" he asked, as he walked toward me with a solemn expression.

"Lila Maclean."

"Oh, good. I was going to come looking for you next. I'm Detective Ortiz." He glanced down at a pad in his hand. "Dr. Salton said you were the only other person who saw the victim in the study. Can you walk me through it, please?"

I gave him my statement and filled out the necessary paperwork. He thanked me and said they'd be in touch if they had any additional questions. His manner was intense and mostly inscrutable with a hint of suspicion. It was nothing like dealing with Stonedale police, who not only knew me through Lex but also from having been involved in several previous cases. They accepted me on a professional level, more or less.

Then again, when I'd first met Lex, he was taking my statement at the scene of a crime, and his demeanor back then had also made me feel guilty even though I was innocent, so perhaps that was just how it was supposed to be.

I shook my head to clear the memories. I didn't want to make any more comparisons to Lex because I didn't want to think about him at all. My heart was still too tender for that. We'd dated on and off for years, then his wife, from whom he'd been separated when he met me, came back into the picture.

I hadn't even known about Helena until she showed up last spring and went after him. She was gorgeous, persuasive, and relentless. After a while, she had convinced him that they deserved to give things a second chance. Helena had made sure to let me know, in the most gloating manner possible. She'd staged—I was convinced—a "chance" encounter at the supermarket in order to let it drop that they were moving to Seattle together. Lex had called and come by at least ten times after Helena's bombshell, but I'd refused to talk to him. Later, I'd received a letter postmarked Seattle and returned it, unopened.

That was that. I hadn't seen it coming, and I wasn't over it yet.

Not that he was a bad guy.

Quite the opposite.

If he hadn't had a wife, he'd have been darn close to perfect.

When I came in to breakfast the next morning, Bibi was in the dining room staring out the window, a cup of tea in hand. A piece of untouched dry wheat toast sat on a plate nearby.

I slid into a nearby chair, setting down my satchel and coffee gently so as not to jolt her or interrupt her thoughts. She looked exhausted. I hadn't been able to sleep the night before, either. I'd tossed and turned, mulling things over in my mind, but I couldn't make any sense of what had happened to Gillian.

"I would say good morning, but it's not a very good one at all, is it?" Her eyes remained fixed on the frozen surface of Silver Rush Lake. It was a thin layer, barely a crust, but it looked deceptively solid in the wintry landscape. The bridge over the far end was covered with snow as well. It was a picturesque scene, far more beautiful than seemed possible given what had happened here last night.

"I'm so sorry, again, for your loss." We'd talked briefly before retiring for bed, and I'd expressed my deepest condolences, but she had been in shock, I was sure. For all I knew, she was still in shock. "Can I get you something? Refresh your tea, perhaps?"

"No, thank you." Her voice was quieter than usual. She lifted the tea without breaking her gaze, took a sip, then set it back into the saucer. "Though I would be grateful if you could help me figure out who killed Gillian."

I choked on my coffee. "The police are working on it..."

"I know. But I can't sit around *waiting*." She finally shifted her eyes to meet mine. "Forgive me if this is a bit too Agatha-Christie-esque, me sipping tea and inviting you to sleuth on my behalf. But I know you've been involved in several cases, and, after all, I saw you in action at Tattered Star Ranch."

"I would very much like to help you, Bibi. But the other times, I was already immersed in the various situations because of circumstances, and it was more natural to—"

"Investigate? Exactly. So how is this any different? You were involved in the situation then; you're involved in the situation now. You found a body then; you found a body now."

"Penelope did, actually," I reminded her.

"Still." She tapped the table. "You know the town. You know my friends. You know this house. And most importantly, you know I need your help."

Her pleading hit a nerve. And the truth was, I could hardly say no. She'd let me stay at Callahan House for months during my sabbatical, free of charge.

I owed her.

"Of course I'll help, Bibi. As much as I can. Together, perhaps our efforts will lead somewhere."

Her shoulders sagged in relief. "Thank you, Lila. I can't tell you how much better I feel already, hearing you say that."

She added jam to her toast while I dug around in my satchel for a pen and paper to take notes. One hazard of a teaching job was the powerful tendency to want to inscribe things on paper, so I kept them close at hand.

I jotted down the date, then looked up at Bibi. "Ready to begin?"

She shifted slightly in her chair. "Yes."

"How long have you known Gillian?"

"First day of kindergarten. She was behind me in line, tapped my shoulder, and handed me a piece of taffy. That captures her, really. She was always sweet." Her eyes filled with tears, and she dabbed at her face with a cloth napkin. "We were fast friends from that day forward."

"Did she live near you?"

"Close enough that we could ride our bikes." Bibi paused. "Not sure if I mentioned it, but my family lived in one of the guest cottages here. The one you've been staying in, actually."

I stared at her.

"At Callahan House? I thought you moved in after you married Jamison."

"No. We were on the estate long before that. Not when we first moved to Larkston, but soon after, when my stepfather left us." Her lips twisted. "He was an insurance man and provided for us well enough, but my mother wasn't the type to put up with any nonsense. He was a nasty sort in general and a philanderer to boot. She found out that he had cheated on her, and from that point on, she made her displeasure known daily in all sorts of ways. Eventually, he fled. No one was sad to see him go, and in fact we never saw him again, but it meant my mother needed to find work. As luck would have it, the Callahans were looking for a live-in cook. She made a delicious meal for them as an application and got the job."

"And that's when you met your husband?"

"Yes." Her eyes fell on their wedding picture hanging on the wall. They made a striking couple. "Though I never would have guessed that Jamie and I would later date, much less end up married. It all began one day when I went to climb a tree by the lake, where I planned to read the latest Nancy Drew book. He was there, perched in my favorite spot, reading the Hardy Boys. We started talking about mysteries and ended up trading books—and we never stopped until the day he and Hudson went off the road into the lake. Right near that bridge."

She inclined her head toward the window.

"I'm so sorry, Bibi."

"Thank you. It's been years, but sometimes I still expect him to come through the door, waving a new book around, wanting me to read it. He was fanatical when he fell in love with someone's work. He'd talk about it for days on end." Bibi considered me. "You know, Jamie would have liked you very much, Lila, and joined into our literature discussions with gusto. I've enjoyed it so much myself. Retirement has been too quiet. At first, it was a relief to get out of the classroom—all of those papers to be graded surging toward you like a never-ending tidal wave—but I do miss the deep conversations we had and the wonderful insights of my students. There is nothing like analyzing a story and sharing discoveries with someone who has read it as closely as you have."

"Confession time: I don't want to leave."

She laughed. "I don't want you to leave, either. But your students will be glad you're back."

"That's kind of you to say."

"I know you're putting the final touches on your book, or I suppose I should say books, plural? We have talked about the Dare study—forgive me for referring to it in third person but sometimes it's easier to compartmentalize—and it sounds like you'll be submitting that soon."

"Fingers crossed."

"How is your novel coming along?"

I laughed. "The manuscript has been revised a few times. I'm not sure what to do with it next."

"You should have people read it now, see what they think. Gillian would have been the first to offer," she said softly. "She was fond of you and very supportive of new mystery writers. Which brings us back to her. Sorry that I wandered away."

"It's fine. Did Gillian have any enemies?"

"She was universally loved—and she deserved that. She was the first to volunteer when someone needed help. A compassionate soul through and through."

"Did she and Hudson have any children?"

"No. They wanted them—Jamie and I did too—but it never happened. Since Margot and Win had two children and Penelope and Brody had four, we were able to be doting godparents at least."

I nodded. "Can you tell me more about her work? Anyone she might have unintentionally crossed there?"

"She was a literary agent for decades. She hit it big with some of her earliest clients, opened up the Shane Literary Agency in Denver and was extremely successful. I think she had about twenty agents working for her when she retired. But she always had time to give advice to new authors."

"Could there have been someone who wanted to work with her agency and was rejected? Or someone she may have clashed with while doing business?"

"Of course that's always possible, but I never heard of anyone who was angry after an interaction with Gillian."

I made a note to contact her agency, see if they'd speak to me.

Tears welled up in Bibi's eyes again. "When Jamie and Hudson died, it was harder for Gillian in some ways, I think, because Hudson was driving. She felt responsible. I told her that she wasn't, but we do tend to cling to our beliefs once we commit to them. No one knows what happened that night. They missed the bridge somehow. There was ice, there was a lake, there was an accident."

"Was it snowing?"

"Yes. A horrible blizzard. But there was also suspicion that someone forced them off the road. It was never proven."

"Oh, Bibi. That's tragic."

"Indeed. His parents didn't last much longer after that."

"That's when you inherited Callahan House?"

"Yes. Jamie had an older brother, Jensen, but he left home when we were in high school. Some kind of falling out with his father, who was a rigid sort. No one has heard from him since."

"I see."

She gripped the table. "Lila, what if one of my guests did this, hurt Gillian?"

It was a sobering thought. "Yes, or someone else could have snuck in. Was the back door unlocked?"

"Probably. I leave it open so that Alice and Darien can come and go." The Flemms had worked for the Callahans forever, according to Bibi; Alice, who worked as a housekeeper, was married to Darien, the groundskeeper. The Flemms lived in the second guest cottage between the main house and the lake. Darien stayed outside for the most part, but Alice was often inside. I'd run into her numerous times, though she hadn't given me more than a curt greeting and a curious look. She always seemed to be gliding through the hallway silently, a feather duster in her hand. I'd nearly jumped out of my skin the first time I'd unexpectedly encountered her in the shadows.

Bibi had confided to me that she didn't require a housekeeper, but she hadn't had the heart to let Alice and Darien go after Jamie died. Their family had lived on the property longer than she had, and as far as Bibi was concerned, they could live there as long as they wanted, even if they never did a single thing to help out. She made sure they knew that, too.

But Alice did what she liked, and apparently she liked to dust.

"You might want to change things up," I said quietly. "Ask them to use their keys instead of leaving the door unlocked. Considering what just happened."

Bibi thought about this, chewing her lip. "Yes, that's a good idea."

There was a muffled sound, as if a door had been banged shut. I looked at Bibi questioningly.

She listened for a moment, then pointed toward the front of

the house. "I think Alice is in the parlor right now."

"I usually don't hear her come and go."

"Neither do I."

"Does Alice talk to you? She doesn't talk to me."

Bibi leaned forward. "She has *spoken* to me. In short sentences. I wouldn't say that we've had extended conversations."

"How long have you known her?"

"She was a few years ahead of me in school."

I tried to hide my shock. Alice seemed eons older than Bibi.

"Her parents and my mother worked for the Callahans, and we all lived in our respective cottages. She never liked me much, though."

"I can't believe there's anyone alive who wouldn't like you."

Bibi shrugged. "We never got off on the right foot. They were here first...I don't know. We didn't click."

"Even now, when you're letting them live here?"

Bibi lowered her voice even more. "I don't believe they see the situation as me *letting* them live here. They don't view me as a real Callahan."

"But you are."

"Only by marriage."

"Which absolutely *counts*." My indignation was reflected in my tone.

"Thank you." She winked at me. "Before you go, Lila, I've been meaning to ask you something: would you let me read your manuscript?"

"Oh, you have too much going on for that." I demurred, not knowing which book she meant but not wanting to impose in either case. "I wouldn't dream of it."

"I'd like to read the mystery first, please," she continued, as if reading my mind. "Then, if you're willing, the critical study."

"That's unbelievably kind and utterly terrifying."

Now she laughed. "I understand completely. I know it's scary, but it can also be helpful. Don't say no yet. Think about it. In the meantime, you might want to start joining some of the professional groups for authors."

"But I've not published a book."

"Yet. But you've *written* a book. Two even. You belong. Oh, and wait until you go to a mystery conference. You'll be giddy."

"Isn't it like an academic conference?" I'd been to many of those and never for a moment felt giddy. Not to say that they weren't enjoyable—as intellectual activities go, they could be stimulating and energizing—I'd met Bibi at a conference, after all. But most academic gatherings were infused with a palpable sense of hierarchy and judgment that required strong maintenance of the expected professional demeanor.

"Yes, except the prevailing mood is joyful. The last time I attended one, the person at the registration desk told me that she's seen a lot of conferences held in their hotel but that she likes the mystery readers and writers best because they're so obviously pleased to be there."

"I'll add it to my bucket list."

"You must. I regretted that once I became a professor, I left that all behind. Don't make the same mistakes I did. You can do both."

"It's not too late for you to rejoin, is it?"

"I don't know if I'll ever be Isabella Dare again outside of these walls." She straightened up. "Good luck finding Alice."

Alice proved easier to find than I'd expected, as she was drifting down the hallway right outside the kitchen where we were talking, a location amenable to eavesdropping.

It could have been a coincidence.

I greeted her and she floated away faster, the feathers waving on the duster as if they were saying goodbye for her. With a few quick steps, I'd caught up and said her name again. She finally stopped trying to escape, turning to face me, and I took in her general sense of disarray. Her puff of white hair launched in all directions at once above her deeply lined face, she'd missed a button on her taupe sweater, and the hem of her mud-colored skirt was crooked.

"Hello, Alice. Bibi wanted me to ask you a few questions." I threw that last part in about Bibi authorizing things because I knew she wouldn't have spoken to me otherwise.

Her eyes narrowed but she didn't respond.

"Did you happen to see anyone other than the book club guests here last night? Or did you see anything odd or out of place?"

Her glare didn't waver. After two full minutes of silence, I gave up.

"If you think of anything unusual that you may have seen, could you please tell me? Or Bibi. We're trying to figure out what happened to Gillian."

She returned to her goal of moving away from me.

"Thank you," I called after her.

I'd have to let Bibi take over if there were future interrogations involving Alice. If it were anyone else, I'd probably find it peculiar that she had nothing to say to me, but it was very much in keeping with the strange, ghostly presence I'd lived with all fall.

If she was happy haunting Callahan House, who was I to say anything?

Chapter 4

Since my conversation with Alice had gone exactly nowhere, I decided to check on the state of the study. I didn't know if Bibi had gone inside after they'd taken Gillian away, but if she hadn't, I wanted to clean up any mess. She was already grieving, and I didn't want her to happen upon something that made things worse.

The police had been here until the early morning hours. They hadn't put up any crime scene tape or told us to stay out of the room. Detective Ortiz said they had already gotten what they needed. The door was ajar, so I gave it a push. When it swung open slowly, I was surprised to see that aside from powder where they'd dusted for fingerprints, the room looked basically the same. I don't know what I'd been expecting, but it wasn't normality. That in and of itself was surreal, and goosebumps broke out on my arms. After sending up positive thoughts for Gillian, I took a deep breath and crossed to the windows. As I yanked the curtains apart to bring more light into the room, they swept back to reveal an item lying next to the wall: a silver key.

I caught my breath, recognizing the scrolled design on the top. Gillian hadn't given it back to Bibi, as she'd agreed to do.

I moved quickly to the desk, testing the handle of the drawer where the manuscript had been. I expected it to be locked. Instead, it slid open, revealing that the drawer was empty.

* * *

I ran around the house until I found Bibi, who was sitting in the library next to the fire. Her fingers flew over the keyboard of her laptop on the small table in front of her.

"I'm sorry to interrupt you, but do you have the manuscript?"

Bibi looked at me over her rectangular glasses. "Which manuscript, dear?"

"The one from your study."

"*The Secrets of Everwell*? No, I haven't seen it in years. I'd completely forgotten it was in there until you mentioned it last night. Why?"

"It's gone."

She stared at me for an uncomfortable moment.

"Oh, Lila, are you sure?"

"The drawer was unlocked and empty."

"I'm calling the police. Maybe they took it." She pulled out her cell phone and dialed. I sank down in the chair next to her. After she reported the state of things, she disconnected. "They didn't remove the manuscript, and they'll be here soon."

"I'm sorry it's gone, Bibi."

She stood and began pacing back and forth. "No one must ever see that book."

"Why not?"

"I was careless."

"About what?"

"I wrote about a tragedy. It was my way of processing it."

"What's wrong with that?"

Bibi sighed. "I was extremely angry. I speculated about who was responsible for this event without anything to support those claims."

"But it's fiction."

"Yes, but it's very much based on something that happened in reality. Anyone who lived here then and knows the story will be able to recognize the characters. It could ruin their lives."

"What happened?"

She returned to her chair and stared at the fire for a long time. I'd begun to think she wasn't going to respond until she spoke so softly, I had to lean forward to hear her. "We had decided to have a bonfire down at the lake—Margot, Penelope, Gillian, and I. As I think I've mentioned, the four of us started calling ourselves the Larks in grade school. It was a silly thing, but it stuck."

Bibi closed her laptop and turned to face me. "We did that a lot—had bonfires. Jamie's parents didn't mind. They let him run wild as long as he earned excellent grades. He would be going to Callahan College, obviously, but they wanted him to shine and perhaps even go on to graduate school. After Jensen left, they were too afraid of scaring off another son, I think, to put too many limitations on him, even though it was obvious that they were watching him more closely."

"That must have been difficult."

"Jamie handled it well. He had the most even-keeled personality—nothing really fazed him. Anyway, we set up chaise lounges and blankets borrowed from Callahan House, and our boyfriends showed up when it got dark. College was starting soon, so it was our last night of summer. It was perfect at first, as those things go—talking, laughing, celebrating our transition. We all drank too much, though, and things got a little blurry. At some point, Winston, Brody, Hudson, and Jamie took off into the woods. They wanted to do something, I can't remember what. Swing from trees, chase rabbits, look for gold—who knows. I was tired, so I went home. Hours later, my mother woke me in a state, saying that my sister Ilse was missing."

I gasped.

"My mother had thought Ilse was at a sleepover—the first she'd ever agreed to attend, actually, as she was a bit of a loner—but when Mom went to pick her up, they said Ilse had left sometime during the night. They hadn't realized it until morning. So everyone was looking for her. I went out with my friends and combed the woods. We set up sort of a command post at the diner in town. My mother went over to the Callahans', waiting for news. She sat with them all day and night. And for several more days and nights. But there was no news. My sister just never came home. My mother died later that year. She went so quickly. It was as if her heart just broke."

"Oh, Bibi." I went over and hugged her. "I'm so sorry."

"Thank you." Her voice trembled slightly. "Not knowing what happened to Ilse made it difficult not to be suspicious of everyone I knew and loved, in some ways, after that. And I wrote the book—which was the first time I developed the character of Athena Bolt, by the way—in order to exorcise some of those feelings about having been out enjoying myself with friends while who knows what happened to my sister. I felt tremendously guilty. In the process of channeling that into a murder mystery, I worked out some of my other frustrations about the dynamics of that group."

"Which were?"

She made a small sound of dismissal. "The usual things people worry about in high school, I suppose. Small dramas, in retrospect."

"Did you have a theory about what happened to Ilse?"

"I made some guesses. But they were wild ones initially, out of anger and pain. The book was never meant to be seen. How did you even find it?"

"The key was lying on the carpet underneath the desk. But I put the manuscript back in the drawer after I saw it, and I'm positive it was locked. I was going to give you the key myself, but after you fainted, I was in the kitchen with Gillian, who insisted that she be the one to bring it back to you. You've said over and over again that you trust the Larks implicitly, so I didn't even think twice about it. I should have been more careful."

"There was no reason not to give it to Gillian. She would have brought the key to me eventually."

"But..." I stopped. Maybe now wasn't the time to cast aspersions.

"Go ahead, please, Lila."

"But it looks like she went into your study and unlocked the drawer with it instead."

Bibi smiled sadly. "She was a literary agent. I imagine she thought she could do something for me. I probably wouldn't have been able to resist either, if the tables were turned."

"She didn't represent Isabella Dare—"

"No. But once the proverbial cat was out of the bag—"

My cheeks flushed. "I'm sorry, again."

"What's done is done. However, to be crystal clear, I trust the Larks with my secrets. We have been best friends our entire lives. The information is not going to go anywhere—don't worry, Lila." She paused, thinking. "You did mention the title when you told the group about the book, right?"

"*The Secrets of Everwell*? Yes."

"It would have meant something to them. 'Everwell' is what we called the place where we had our bonfires. Someone had dubbed it that in the beginning, joking that no matter what happened, things would be 'ever well' as long as we were together at the lake. Gillian would have expected that the book included our little adventures from that time period. I imagine her curiosity got the better of her."

"Do you think that's why someone attacked her? To get the manuscript?" I asked it as gently as I could.

"Since the manuscript is missing, that does make sense."

"Do you have any other copies?"

"No. I typed it on a portable Smith Corona and didn't use carbon paper. That was in the seventies, long before people had their own computers—or copiers, for that matter. I did hold onto the original pages, though, and once Jamie and I moved into Callahan House, I found it among my school papers. That was when I locked the manuscript in the drawer because I didn't want anyone else to read it. I thought maybe after some years had passed, I might be able to revisit and rework it into something, but once I started teaching, I didn't write fiction anymore. Eventually, I forgot it was even there."

"Where did you keep the key?"

She frowned. "It was in a little hollow underneath the desk, where the top met the back. I taped it in there quite securely, but it must have fallen."

"Maybe over the years, the tape adhesive wore down."

"Unfortunately."

We both fell silent. After a moment, I reached out and touched her arm. "Is there anything I can get for you?"

"No, thank you. But I think I'll go make some coffee to offer to the police when they arrive."

Before she left the room, she looked back over her shoulder. "Where did you find the key the second time around?"

"Near the desk, under the curtains. She must have unlocked the drawer, set down the key, and pulled out the manuscript. Whoever took the pages wouldn't have needed the key since she'd already used it."

"Why wouldn't the police have taken the key as evidence?"

"Maybe they didn't see it. Maybe it was dropped and kicked under the curtain by mistake...or hidden there intentionally. But now that I think about it, could the killer have taken the key away from her before she got to the drawer?"

"I think it's far more likely that Gillian did use the key. There's not much on this green earth that could've stopped her from getting to a potential literary acquisition if she had an interest. She could be impressively fierce when she needed to be. And she definitely would not have told anyone else about the manuscript if she was going to look for it, either. That would have generated competition. Although I don't want to dwell upon what her final moments were like, I imagine that the killer ripped the manuscript right out of Gillian's hands." Bibi shook her head sadly. "Either way, I'm glad you're going to help sort this out. You've already made a substantial discovery."

I nodded miserably, wishing I'd never told Gillian about the key in the first place. Would she have been killed if she hadn't been in possession of the manuscript, if that's what had happened?

How much of this was my fault?

The guest cottage where I was staying was located in the woods behind the main house on the right, parallel to the other cottage where Alice and Darien lived on the left. It was necessary to take a path to go from one to another, and the surrounding pines made each one feel secluded. You could barely make out the others in the triangle of buildings through the tree branches.

My cottage was shaped like something out of a fairy tale, with a sharply pitched roof, an arched door and windows, and a perfectly maintained box hedge along the front. Inside, there was a tiny kitchen dominated by an old drop-leaf table and a charming main room with a sofa, television, and fireplace. A very small hallway led to two bedrooms—one of which was set up as a study with a large wooden desk, chair, and printer stand—and a bathroom with a modern sink and shower. I had enjoyed the space during my sabbatical and would miss it when I returned to Stonedale.

As the snow fell, I was curled up by the fire with my laptop, doing some revisions. When Bibi knocked on my door after talking to the police, I offered her a cup of cocoa. She waved that away and perched on a chair at the kitchen table, pointing to a painting on the far wall that had a cheerful cluster of red and blue flowers. There was something joyful in the composition. "Sorry about the art."

"I love that one—it always lifts my spirits. Who's the artist?"

She wrinkled her nose. "Guilty."

"Oh! You're talented."

"I wish that were true. It was a paint-by-number kit, if I remember correctly. Anyway, sorry to intrude, but I didn't feel like being alone in the house all day after..." she shivered.

"I understand."

She brushed something off of the table. "Do you want to go into town, maybe have dinner?"

"Sure. I'm doing some research but could leave in an hour or so. And you'd be welcome to stay here while I work—"

"Oh no," she said. "I only wanted to line something up for later. As long as I know I'll be leaving the grounds, that makes me feel better. I live in the house, after all. I'm going to have to get used to it, crime scene or not."

A muffled alert sound came from her pocket. She pulled out her cell and read it, her jaw dropping.

"What's going on?"

She turned the phone around so that I could read the screen: "Callahan Curse Strikes Again!"

Chapter 5

Everything changed in an instant. Bibi said we needed to go into Larkston right away. I drove while she busily texted—her phone pinged over and over again with incoming messages. Once we reached the main street, she told me to park in front of Cherry's Diner, a white brick building with a sign over the front door spelling out the name of the restaurant in perky neon cursive. Bibi asked the hostess for her regular booth and informed me that the Larks would soon be meeting us.

"Is this the only diner in town?" I asked.

She nodded approvingly. "That was a tactful way of asking if this was the diner where we met up with the boys after Ilse went missing. And yes."

I looked around at the red vinyl booths, the black-and-white-checkered floor tiles, and the jukebox at the far end near the rectangular pick-up window. Although the diner had been here for years, there was a freshness to the decor. "It looks almost new."

"They spiffed everything up a few years ago. When we used to come here in high school, the floors were already scuffed, and the seats had seen much better days. It's the original jukebox, though." She dug through her purse and pulled out a dime. "Want to play something? I like D-7, myself."

I walked to the glass beast—it was almost as tall as I was—and put in the coin, then hit the button that flipped the catalog of available songs until I landed on D-7. The machine made a metallic grumble, and a rack of records spun around behind the glass, coming to a stop with a loud clank. I couldn't see the needle land on the vinyl, but I heard it make contact with a faint crackle. As the familiar sounds of "These Boots Are Made for Walkin'" by Nancy Sinatra began, I returned to Bibi, who was deep in conversation with Margot and Penelope.

After sliding into the circular booth, I greeted the women and they all smiled, though it seemed relatively strained.

"We ordered for you," Margot declared from her spot between Bibi and Penelope. "We're having coffee and cherry pie. It's the house specialty."

Before I had a chance to respond, Bibi slid her phone over to me. "Read this article—it's the one with the headline I showed you earlier."

I scanned the text, absorbing the information as quickly as I could. The first half gave details about Gillian's murder in somewhat sensationalistic terms. I said as much to the group.

"It's Tacey's style," Margot said, with an almost imperceptible snort. "She's the most theatrical person I've ever met."

I bet my mother—known to her adoring fans as the artist Violet O—could give her a run for her money. She tended toward the performative end of the scale. If pressed, I would have admitted that I rather liked her shenanigans. Most of the time.

"Sorry, I should have clarified. I meant Tacey Throckham," Margot went on. "Her father owned the old newspaper, which was called *The Larkston Courier*. Bequeathed it to her. Once she got her hands on it, she closed up shop on the printing presses and went digital. Turned it into what amounts to a gossip blog, *Larkston Live*, with news coverage that is far more subjective than objective. High on Tacey's opinion, low on verified facts."

"Don't call it a blog, though. She'll rake you through the coals.

She still thinks of herself as a hardcore reporter. We all have learned to take it with more than a grain of salt," Penelope said.

"Keep reading." Bibi pointed to her phone. "*Larkston Live* is more outrageous than usual today."

"Industrial-strength crazy," Margot said.

The second half of the post pointed out that Gillian's demise, Jamie and Hudson's accident, and Ilse's disappearance had all happened on the same property and gave a brief recap of each tragedy. Tacey ended the article by inviting readers to speculate about what would happen next.

"Wow," I said, handing Bibi her phone. "That's unbelievable."

"Ridiculous. Just because things happened to the same family doesn't mean they're cursed," Penelope said. "Haven't the Callahans suffered enough?"

"It's absurd," Margot agreed angrily. "Why does she have to turn people's suffering into something trashy?"

"I'm so sorry," I said to Bibi. It felt as though all I'd done in the past week was tell her that I was sorry for things she had lost. There had been so many. My heart ached for her.

A smiling server with a towering beehive hairdo and a pencil stuck behind her ear swept up with our order. After she unloaded the pies from her round tray, she poured steaming coffee into our cups, then set a silver creamer jug and a bowl of sugar cubes in the center of the table. "Will that do it for now?"

When no one requested anything, a look of relief crossed her face and she left.

I cut a small bite of the golden pie, being sure to run my fork through the dollop of whipped cream on top. It was warm, sweet, and exactly the kind of food I hadn't even known I'd needed. We ate in silence until the pies were gone. The slices were so delicious that there wasn't any other option.

I poured a splash of cream into my coffee and took a sip. Also heavenly. No wonder this place had been in business since the mid-twentieth century.

For the first time in a long time, I felt focused, if only momentarily.

I addressed Bibi. "Is there anything we can do? Would it do any good to talk to Tacey? I have no idea what she's like, but if you want her to stop with the curse thing, maybe she'll listen?"

"You're about to find out what she's like," Margot muttered, pointing at the woman huffing across the diner in our direction. Her substantial frame was enclosed in a long green coat, and a capacious handbag was slung over one shoulder. On her short, meticulously curled hair rode a hat from which a single peacock feather sprouted a foot into the air. A lace scarf was draped across her shoulders. All in all, she looked like she'd stepped out of an earlier era.

Not what I'd expected from a digital diva.

"Hello, ladies," Tacey said in a manner just short of a trill. "I trust you saw my story today? I'd love to join you and get some details for my follow-up article."

Penelope edged toward the place where the booth seat ended so that Tacey couldn't sit there.

"Stop right there." Margot held her hand up in Tacey's direction, palm out. "We don't have anything to say to you."

Tacey smirked. "Of course you do. Let me run some facts by you." She stepped over to my side and sat on the edge of the booth. To my horror, she began wiggling with her lower half, pushing me toward Bibi.

I held my ground for the most part, and eventually she stopped playing human bumper cars and stretched out her legs instead to brace herself firmly into the tiny territory she'd conquered.

Bibi sighed. "Could you please stop calling it the Callahan

Curse, Tacey?"

She shrugged. "I don't think so. It's been out there for a while."

"But—"

"What in heaven's name is going on over there?" Tacey lumbered on. "Not that I'm accusing you of anything, but three *is* a pattern."

"Shut up!" Margot glared at Tacey. "Don't you know that Bibi's in pain? That we are all in pain? We've lost a dear friend and all you can do is try to capitalize on that to score hits on your blog. You should be *ashamed* of yourself."

Tacey tsked. She opened the clasp of her purse and dug around inside.

Margot rolled her eyes and threw up her hands.

"Come now, Margot. I'm sorry for your loss. I thought Gillian was a nice person. That's why I'm trying to honor her story." Tacey pulled out a small tape recorder, then delivered the next part in a rush. "But we're not in high school anymore, and you can't boss us all around."

Margot leaned forward and tapped the table with an elegant finger. "We may not be in high school anymore, but how about this? I'm a friend of the *mayor*. He listens to my ideas. Maybe one of my ideas could be that we need someone to hold our reckless town paper accountable for printing false stories. Come to think of it, we might need to launch an investigation. Or a lawsuit."

Tacey gaped at her, then got ahold of herself. "You wouldn't dare."

"Wouldn't I? I think you know me better than that," Margot purred.

Tacey pursed her lips, then turned to Bibi, holding out her tape recorder. "Here's your chance to get your side of things out into the world. What do you want readers to know?"

Bibi remained silent.

"Last chance." Tacey shook the tape recorder at her. "You'll be sorry if you don't take this opportunity."

"Lila, push her out of the booth right now!" Margot snapped at me.

"Never mind," Tacey said angrily, scrambling up, which took considerable effort. "I'll call you later."

"I'm still not going to talk to you, Tacey," Bibi spoke evenly. "You've done enough harm to my family."

"Suit yourself, but the offer stands, Bibi. We both know you're going to need me someday." Tacey huffed away from us, her peacock feather bouncing.

"Sorry about my behavior just now," Margot said through gritted teeth. "I cannot stand that woman. She brings out the worst in me. Always has."

"Think she got the message," Penelope said. "And I can't believe she's wearing a peacock feather."

"At least it's fake," Margot said. "Like she is."

Bibi waved her hands. "We have another issue, Larks: *The Secrets of Everwell* is missing."

Margot and Penelope stared at her.

"In it, I described the night that Ilse disappeared in detail and made some guesses about what happened to my sister."

"What's your conclusion?" Penelope pressed Bibi.

"It wasn't anything I'd say out loud now. By writing it, I worked out a hypothetical theory."

"Now you *have* to say," Penelope said. "We haven't talked about that night in decades—"

"Pen," Margot warned. "Stop."

Penelope stopped.

"Why wouldn't you talk—" I began.

"Margot means that we should focus on Gillian now," Bibi said hastily. "But that's precisely why I'm bringing this up, Larks. Even if it doesn't lead to anything, I've asked Lila to help me."

I nodded. "Since the manuscript was the last thing Gillian may have touched before it went missing, I'm pursuing the angle that the content may be important. It would be helpful to hear your perspectives about the night that Ilse disappeared. She's already told me some of what she remembers."

They exchanged a look that was, to me, impenetrable.

"Individually," I added. "Not here."

Bibi did something with her hands—some sort of Larks signal—and they both agreed. We made arrangements for me to visit them in the next few days.

I made a mental note to speak more with Bibi too. I'd realized later that while she had given me the general gist of the events, she hadn't explained exactly what it was that people would be embarrassed about if the manuscript were to be published. Other than high school drama. And whoever she blamed for Ilse's disappearance.

"I bet we'll all remember it the same way," Penelope said slowly, her eyes on Margot as if expecting to be shushed again. When Margot remained silent, her speed increased. "We talked so much back then, it's probably blurred into one story in our minds."

"I understand how witnesses who compare notes often form a narrative that accounts for gaps, but still, there may be some specific details that are summoned by the individual expression of the story," I replied.

"I wrote about it not long after we all discussed it," Bibi said. "Even so, doing that allowed me to come to a different conclusion than what we all may have discussed collectively. You may too, in your own retelling."

"What about our husbands?" Margot asked.

Bibi considered this. "I suppose Lila will need to find out what they remember too. They were there, after all. But please impress upon them the importance of keeping the existence of the manuscript—as well as the fact that I am the one who wrote it—a secret."

"And could you please not talk about it with each another again until I've had a chance to chat with you one on one?" It felt strange saying that, as if I were playing detective.

Then again, I guess I was.

Chapter 6

On the drive back to Callahan House, I tried to elicit more information from Bibi, but she asked if we could talk at another time. She was tired, she said, and the jaunt into town had taken more out of her than she'd expected.

Although I was disappointed, I wanted to respect her wishes. She was grieving.

But I'd circle back later for sure.

Since we hadn't eaten dinner, I offered to make something. My culinary skills were limited, but I could throw together a simple meal. She agreed to meet me in an hour and went off to lie down.

I headed into the kitchen to construct an edible dinner, come what may.

"This is delicious, Lila." Bibi put down her spoon and smiled at me. "Very restorative."

I'd been lucky and found some boxed squash soup that only required heating. I'd also cut up some crusty bread and made grilled cheese sandwiches. Not fancy by any stretch of the imagination, but it was warm and filling. I'd set tray tables in the parlor, near the fireplace, and our dining experience was downright cozy.

The hallway door opened and Alice slipped in, followed by her husband Darien, who towered over her, a baseball hat in hand. They both bent slightly forward, as if bracing themselves against an invisible wind. At the sight of us, they paused and turned to go, mumbling apologies.

"No, wait! Have you eaten? We have plenty of soup," I said. "I'd be glad to make you a sandwich too."

"We've already had our dinner," Darien said. "But that's mighty kind of you. Appreciate the hospitality." I was struck by how tidy he was, compared to his wife—his flannel shirt and jeans had been pressed. His gray hair was cut short and combed neatly, though a small dent from where his hat must have spent the day was visible. Meanwhile, Alice was wearing a thoroughly wrinkled mustard-colored sweater with jeans—and one pant leg was rolled up to her calf while the other one wasn't. Her socks had smiling green spiders on them.

"Why don't you come in for some cocoa at least? I was just about to make some." As the words came out of my mouth, I realized that I may have crossed some sort of line regarding their routine. I'd never seen them eat with Bibi or do anything together, come to think of it. Alice and Darien were on the property but kept to themselves for the most part.

I shot an apologetic look at Bibi, but she was waving her hand at the empty chairs nearby. "Please, do."

They hesitated for a moment then moved forward slowly.

I gathered up the bowls, plates, and silverware and took them into the kitchen, where I put the kettle on. As the water warmed, I collected four stoneware mugs, poured in the cocoa mix, and arranged several marshmallows in a small bowl for each person so they could add, or not, as desired. By the time I returned to the parlor, Bibi and Darien were talking intently. Their voices weren't raised but I could sense the tension between them starting to increase.

"I don't know what to do," Bibi said.

Darien's eyebrows drew together. "Whatever is necessary. Keep them at bay."

"Options are limited." Bibi reached out to take a mug from the tray. Darien and Alice accepted theirs as well.

I sat down next to Bibi and passed the marshmallows. No one else took any, so I took three.

Bibi tasted her cocoa and smiled at me approvingly. "Darien was telling me that the police came by when we were gone."

That's not what I heard, unless the police were the ones who had to be kept at bay, as Darien had described it. That didn't make any sense.

"What did they say?" I looked at Darien, who lifted his mug and slurped down half of his cocoa in one fell swoop. Alice, on the other hand, was taking dainty little sips and smacking her lips in between.

"They, uh, haven't found anything out yet. But they wanted to ask Bibi some questions." He turned his head toward Bibi. "You're supposed to call."

She stood. "If you'll excuse me, I'll go do that right now."

I had the feeling that the conversation I was trying to follow wasn't the same conversation they were actually having. It was as though they were speaking in code.

Darien rose soon afterwards and set his mug on the coffee table. Alice followed suit, giving hers a regretful glance.

"You're welcome to stay," I said, wanting her to be able to savor her drink.

"Thanks all the same," Darien said curtly. He was buzzing with anger—presumably from whatever he and Bibi had been talking about.

I plunged ahead. This was going to be awkward no matter what, so I might as well. "I was hoping to ask you some questions, if you didn't mind."

"I heard about how you interrogated Alice already," Darien said.

"I only asked a few—"

He raised his hand, cutting me off. "We don't know anything about Gillian."

Maybe his anger wasn't directed at Bibi after all.

"Okay. I'm also talking with people about the night Ilse disappeared."

His eyelids closed halfway, like a shade going down. "We have nothing to say about that either."

Alice lifted her chin and refused to look at me.

I watched helplessly as they left through the hallway door.

Chapter 7

I awoke the next morning with a sense of renewed determination. The facts were out there; I had to gather them. Quickly, I showered, dressed, and ate breakfast. After wishing Bibi a nice day, I warmed up my old Honda and moved carefully down the driveway. Margot had asked me to meet her at Callahan College, which wasn't far—Bibi had told me that the family property lines actually touched those of the school grounds—but the roads were still slick after the recent snowfall. I wanted to take my time.

As I drove over the Silver Rush Bridge, I wondered what had happened the night that Jamie and Hudson went off the road. While I didn't subscribe to the idea of a Callahan Curse, I did wonder that so many accidents had plagued her family. Nothing—Tacey's dramatic reporting aside—suggested that the family had been targeted for any reason. In which case, I supposed that bad luck was always an option.

I turned into the main entrance of the small private school. All of the buildings were rectangular red brick and approximately the same size, though some were taller than others. The road curved in an agreeable way, and I followed it past snowy trees and stone walls until I located the sign for Gold Hall. I parked out front and went up the stairs to the first suite, as Margot had directed me. I was surprised to see her sitting at a desk below an engraved "reception" sign. I had imagined her as the kind of woman who had a corner office and a gaggle of assistants who would come running if she crooked a finger.

She greeted me warmly and offered to take my coat. Once that had been stowed away in a nearby closet, she beckoned for me to follow her to the end of a short hallway, where she knocked on a closed door. After someone responded, she turned the handle and walked inside.

Winston Van Brewer sat behind a massive desk in an enormous chair. Whoever had done the decor had taken a chance by selecting what could only be described as a throne. But Winston's formidable size and height fit perfectly. He was tall and quite solid in that way ex-football players can be. He was well-groomed, with wheat-colored hair slicked back with pomade, evoking a sort of Wall Street flair.

"Come in!" He waved me toward one of two studded leather chairs facing his desk. Margot waited until I'd settled into one before she positioned herself in the other and placed her hands in her lap. As always, her posture was perfect. Her model days had clearly made a lasting impact. I tried to match her pose but suspected my core strength would give out before too long. Putting that out of my mind, I thanked them both for seeing me, even though Margot hadn't told me that her husband would be joining us.

"Good morning, Lola," he said heartily.

"Hello, President Van Brewer. It's Lila, actually."

"Sorry. Call me Winston, please. How may I help you?"

I pulled out my notebook and pen and got right to it. "Have you been in this position long?"

Winston twisted his head in an odd way, clearly taken aback. "Yes, for over a decade now."

"He was a dean before this," Margot added proudly.

"And Margot has worked on campus the whole time as well.

Not usually in this office—Olive, my executive assistant, went on maternity leave a bit earlier than expected. You can't fight nature, can you?" He chuckled. "Anyway, Margot agreed to step in until they sort out a temporary replacement. Usually, my wife heads up the Callahan College Alumni Organization. She's a top-notch fundraiser and acquisitions scout, I tell you what."

"Thank you," Margot said, lowering her eyes.

I *knew* she had her own office and staff-at-the-ready somewhere.

"How lucky are we to be together every day?" He gazed at her fondly.

"So proud of you," she murmured. I couldn't make any sense of this decorous Margot. She seemed like an entirely different person than the firecracker who had instructed me to shove Tacey out of the booth at the diner less than twenty-four hours ago.

"Did Margot tell you what we are talking about?"

He lowered his chin in the affirmative.

"So we can speak openly?" I looked at Margot.

"Absolutely. Winston and I have no secrets."

It wasn't what I'd hoped for—I would have preferred to interview each person separately. But I'd take what I could get and, if need be, ask Margot to meet me privately later.

"What can you tell me about Gillian?" I had learned from Lex that starting with an open-ended question could be useful.

Margot's eyes filled with tears. "A dear friend and person. I miss her tremendously."

Winston cleared his throat. "It's a tragedy."

They talked about Gillian's kindness, energy, and business savvy. They offered stories that demonstrated those characteristics. They talked about how extremely happy Gillian and Hudson were together. They repeated what Bibi had told me—there were rumors about Jamie and Hudson having been run off the road. No idea who would have wanted to hurt them, either.

Margot pulled out a tissue and touched it to her eyes. "We have lost too many of our friends."

"Yes, we have," he agreed.

"I'm so sorry for your loss." Once they were both composed and appeared ready to move on, I asked what they could tell me about Bibi's book.

Winston looked blank.

Margot smacked her forehead lightly. "Oh, I forgot to mention that Lila wants us to share our memories of the night that Ilse disappeared. The book that was stolen from Bibi on the night Gillian died was focused on the tragedy, so she's trying to gather as much information as she can to see if there's any connection or if it's perhaps a coincidence."

"I see." He stroked his chin thoughtfully. "You know, up until the moment we heard about Ilse, it was a jolly good evening. Jamie, Hudson, Brody, and I met our girlfriends at the lake. We'd done it a thousand times, gathered around bonfires for some, you know, old-fashioned fun."

I nodded but didn't interrupt.

"Mostly what I remember was sitting around the fire, cracking jokes and letting loose. Ilse wasn't even there, as I recall—it was Bibi, Gillian, Penelope, and my beloved Margot. We drank some beers, had a decent time."

After it became clear that he was done talking, I turned to Margot. "How about you?"

She laughed. "The same. Though I do remember the guys running off into the woods"—she paused and smiled at Winston—"probably to discharge some testosterone buildup."

"Right!" Winston said, snapping his fingers. "Someone challenged us to a race—Jamie, I think it was—to the bridge and back. We all took off at top speed, but it turned out to be a stupid idea because it was pitch-black and you know what that forest is like: once you're inside it, you can't tell which way is which. I could hear the others getting farther away, but I couldn't see anyone. Eventually, I realized that the secret was to stay within sight of the lake, in case you were wondering. Right on the edge of the trees." He slid his hand out smoothly straight in front of him as illustration.

"Did you make it to the bridge?"

"I did."

"Did everyone?"

Winston grinned. "Everyone claimed to have made it, anyway."

There was something in his voice that I couldn't quite interpret. "Do you think someone lied?"

"We all told our truths, I'm sure."

"What did you think about the others?"

"They're like brothers. Jamie and Brody were great guys—"

"Hudson too," Margot murmured.

They exchanged a look.

"I was getting there, my love," Winston finally spoke.

Margot rolled her eyes and addressed me. "Hudson and Winston liked to compete."

He drew back slightly. "I wouldn't say we *liked* to compete."

"They did," Margot told me. "They enjoyed the challenge."

"We were the best of friends, but we found ourselves contending for many of the same..." He flapped his hand around.

"Things." Margot finished his sentence succinctly.

"Like what?" I smiled encouragingly at him.

He conferred with the ceiling. "Sports, I guess."

"Class rank," Margot added.

"Both of us were up for this job." Winston patted the granite name plate on his desk that was engraved *Callahan College*

President.

For the next minute or so, they waxed nostalgic about all of the ways in which Winston had beaten Hudson at every turn during high school, college, and beyond. I wrote down as many as I could.

When they ran out of additional items, they looked at me expectantly.

"Anything else you can remember about that night at Silver Rush Lake?"

They shook their heads.

I closed my notebook. "May I check in with you again if any other questions arise?"

"Of course," Winston said.

"Whatever you need." Margot smiled.

I reminded them to keep the news about the missing manuscript to themselves and thanked them for their time.

Margot led me back to the reception area and retrieved my coat. "We appreciate what you're doing. Gillian deserves justice."

"She does. I can't promise that I'll be able to discover anything useful, though," I said. "I hope I don't let Bibi down."

"Even if you don't find anything new, you're giving her something to focus on. That's something. If you weren't there to discuss potential theories, she'd be alone in that mansion." She shivered. "Has anyone gone into the room since..."

"The study?"

"Yes. I can't fathom wanting to step inside ever again. It's surely haunted. If not by Gillian's spirit, then by negative energy. I've read that places can retain an imprint of traumatic events. Perhaps Bibi should wall it up completely."

"Like in an Edgar Allan Poe story," Winston said jovially, as he dropped a stack of folders onto the reception desk. He caught my eye and tapped his temple. "Right, professor?"

"Except that the person building a wall in a Poe story is

typically the villain," Margot said. "And Bibi's not that."

A beat passed, then we all loudly agreed with Margot, the volume overcompensating for that split second when we had involuntarily entertained the possibility.

It was incomprehensible to imagine that anyone I'd met in Larkston—*especially* Bibi—was capable of ending another person's life.

And yet someone had.

Chapter 8

The snow was melting into torrents that rushed noisily into grates below the sidewalk. It was a temporary phase, as winter in the Rockies was an unpredictable grab bag of hot days, cold days, and everything in between. Thanks to the sunshine beating down on us, the air was warmer, but the wind was still sharp as I walked over to the student union, located in yet another red brick building, like everything else on campus. A row of small pine trees decorated with multicolored ribbons put me in the properly festive mood for my next task: a committee meeting for the college's holiday party. Bibi was hosting the event at Callahan House, which was a time-honored tradition, and I had volunteered my assistance.

Now that I'd finished my sabbatical projects and organized her study, I *should* be returning home. However, it didn't feel right leaving Bibi just yet. I hadn't figured out who had killed Gillian, for one thing. Or found the missing manuscript, for another. If I went back to Stonedale, all of my colleagues would be busy anyway, immersed in the highly stressful end-of-term phase, during which tempers run high. Plus, I'd feel compelled to begin preparing spring classes and submit the work I'd completed this semester to publishers.

Staying put seemed delightful in comparison.

I walked through the doors of the union and found myself in an open space with round tables filled with students as far as the eye could see. Latticed steel railings on every floor formed a square around the atrium, and tall plants added lush greenery. Along the left side was a glass wall through which I could see a cafeteria. The right side was divided into a coffee bar and a store selling numerous items emblazoned with the Callahan College crest.

I went directly to the coffee bar for a much-needed caffeine boost and a shot of warmth. After I ordered, I heard someone calling my name and turned to see Penelope making her way toward me. She had a backpack slung over one shoulder and a pile of books in the other. Her face was red from the wind, her hair was tousled, and the woolen scarf she'd wound around her neck was unravelling on the end. She said hello and asked what I was doing on campus.

"Bibi requested help with the annual party."

She smiled. "I thought you were here to check things out for your presentation."

I froze. "My what?"

Penelope blinked. "Your presentation? The one you agreed to give at the end of your sabbatical? It's scheduled in one of the meeting rooms upstairs."

It came back to me in a flash. She had extended the invitation in August, when the sabbatical stretched out before me, with nothing on the horizon for miles. Stonedale University's requirement to share our sabbatical work with a wider audience had been fresh in my mind at that time.

I'd cheerfully agreed, then promptly forgotten.

She read the realization on my face. "That's my fault for not mentioning it recently. I thought the events committee had been in touch with you?"

When I shook my head, she continued, "Well, that's unfortunate. They began advertising your visit last month."

"I haven't been checking my school emails since Bibi advised me to turn on my auto-reply during sabbatical. They're probably all sitting there." I shuddered, envisioning the accumulation waiting for me the next time I signed in.

"It's not your fault, Lila. I told them you had agreed to come and should have followed up with you." Penelope shrugged. "And if you can't do it..."

A pang of guilt prodded me. "What's the format and when would you like me to come?"

"Before I mess anything else up, let me quickly double check. Would you mind?" She held out the books, which I took, and unzipped her coat to retrieve her phone from the pocket inside. As she scrolled through emails, I looked down at the title of the top book: *Callahan College: A History* by Dana Callahan.

Penelope tapped her screen a few times. "It's scheduled for Saturday night, so you still have a few days to prepare."

I gulped.

She looked apologetic. "It would be a lecture with questions to follow, if you can swing it. No longer than an hour. No need for visuals or anything. Since it's final exams right now, I don't think it would be too large of a crowd. I can still try to cancel..."

I ignored the screaming inside my brain telling me to back out. "No, that's fine. I'll do it."

"Thank you so much, Lila." She held out her arms for the books I was holding.

I handed her the stack. "The one on top looks interesting."

She glanced down. "Oh, that's for Bibi. Her mother-in-law wrote it."

"How interesting."

"I'm sure that it's *not at all* biased," Penelope said, laughing. "Writing a book about the college that bears your family name."

"What were they like, Jamie's parents?"

"They were nice to us," she said.

"Us?"

"The Larks. Some people in town felt differently about them, though. There was always a faction who thought the Callahans were snobby—you know, because their ancestors founded Larkston and whatnot."

"Did that ever lead to problems?"

"Nothing big. No one ever went after them or anything. It was jealousy, mostly. But there wasn't always peace within the family itself..." she trailed off.

"What do you mean?"

Penelope squirmed. "I have nothing negative to say about the Callahans. They were good to me."

"I understand, but I would appreciate anything you can tell me, even if it doesn't seem to be related. The more I know about Gillian and her circle, the better."

She bit her lip. "You should talk to Bibi about it, but I can tell you that Jamie's brother didn't always see eye to eye with his father."

"Ah." I waited, hoping my noncommittal answer would elicit further details, but she appeared to be done. "Do you want me to take the book for Bibi?"

"I'm going to the planning meeting too, so I'll do it. But appreciate the offer." Penelope flashed me a smile. "See you in Rooms 200 A and B above, once you get your coffee."

Two rooms? How big could one committee be?

I hadn't realized the sheer magnitude of the upcoming event. I'd thought it would involve a group of faculty invited to Callahan House for an elegant cocktail party, which was in fact the case, but it was so much more.

Interior decorators and floral designers had pitched ideas in conjunction with the Winter Wonderland theme. High school choirs had competed for the honor of singing on the front steps. Deejays had submitted sample playlists at an alarming rate. Numerous caterers and lighting companies had put in bids to feed the attendees and festoon the mansion, accordingly. This was the Event of The Year in Larkston, and everyone wanted to be a part of it.

There were sub-committees upon sub-committees handling every possible aspect of the party and plenty of last-minute items to discuss. We had made it almost all the way through the agenda—a spirited argument had broken out involving whether chocolate-dipped candy canes were necessary or even desirable and the energetic woman running the meeting with a relentless gavel was pounding away—when the doors burst open and the Van Brewers strolled in.

The gavel-banging stopped immediately, and the leader made a slight bow. "President Van Brewer!"

"Hello, Pat. Just checking in to see how the plans are rolling along, as it were."

"We're doing great," Pat said, gesturing to the rest of the room. "Did you want to say something to the committee?"

"Oh no. Pretend I'm not here. Carry on, please." He leaned against the wall, crossing his arms over his chest, the very picture of high-powered indulgence. Margot was right next to him, her lips curved up in a smile as she scanned the crowd.

The candy-cane hullabaloo was decided with a vote and we quickly made it through the remainder of the items on the list.

Pat asked if there was any additional business and Bibi rose to her feet. "I'm sorry to have to announce that this will be the last time I can host the Winter Wonderland party at Callahan House. I'm putting it on the market immediately afterwards."

A wave of shock rippled through the room, followed by the

buzz of spontaneous conversations. I stared at Bibi, open-mouthed. Pat banged the gavel again.

After waving her hands to quiet the crowd, Bibi went on. "To all of you who have worked so hard this year and every year, I am deeply grateful for your efforts. Let's make this the best party Callahan House has ever seen."

The committee applauded.

Bibi let out a long breath and patted me on the shoulder. "Thank goodness. Let's make a break for it before Pat descends. I love her dearly, but the woman does insist upon her rules, and I'm not up for rehashing who ignored what official procedures tonight. She'll be livid that I didn't run the house sale announcement by her, or at least that she wasn't the first one to hear the news. People around here do like to get a jump on the gossip."

Back at Callahan House, I was unloading the salads I'd bought at the grocery store on the way home when Bibi came into the kitchen, her eyes red-rimmed. I dropped what I was doing and led her into the dining room.

She patted my arm after I pulled out a chair for her. "Don't mind me, dear. Just having a moment."

"What's going on?"

Bibi sat down and sighed. "Telling the committee about the sale was much harder than I'd thought it would be. I suppose I didn't anticipate their reactions, acting as if I'd betrayed them."

"Of course you didn't betray them."

She gazed out the window. "I would understand if they do feel that way. We've hosted the holiday party here for decades, and the college is accustomed to using Callahan House for other events throughout the year as well. It's a longstanding, though informal, agreement. But it's too expensive for me to keep this place up anymore."

"It's not your fault, Bibi."

"I also feel like I'm letting the family down too." She wiped away a tear.

"Surely your husband wouldn't have wanted you to be saddled with an overwhelming financial burden."

"Jamie wouldn't, of course, but his family might consider it my duty to preserve the estate at all costs. After all, they allowed my family to live here for years rent-free. And they allowed me to marry their son."

I touched her hand. "But they're not here anymore. This is *your* home now. You can do whatever you wish."

A door slammed somewhere inside the house.

We both jumped.

"That happens sometimes," Bibi said. "I suspect it means they're unhappy with me."

"The Callahans?"

She nodded.

Chapter 9

Penelope's office matched her general vibe. Stacks of papers dotted the desktop, amidst an assortment of crystals, a miniature bust of Emily Dickinson, and a clay bowl full of paperclips. The walls were covered with literary event posters and photos of flowers at various historical sites. Her framed degrees were lined up on the windowsill, and her bookshelves were bursting with unruly piles teetering on the edge, with titles wedged in sideways along the top in every conceivable space.

The professor herself sat across from me, hands folded in front of her, emanating serenity.

"Thanks for talking to me, Penelope. I won't take up too much of your time."

"Happy to do it. Anything to help figure out what happened to poor Gillian."

"What can you tell me about her?"

"Gillian was kind-hearted, funny, and so smart. I cannot come up with a single example of anyone who might have wanted to hurt her, ever, and we've been close friends since grade school."

I couldn't think of anything else to ask about her friend. In that succinct summary, she'd already covered the important points. "Let's dive into the subject of the missing manuscript—everything you can remember about the night Ilse went missing."

She looked over my shoulder, gathering her thoughts, her dark brown eyes a strong contrast to her pale blonde hair, which was pulled back into a wispy ponytail. Her beige cardigan had interesting knobs of yarn unevenly spaced out. Whether they were there on purpose or by mistake, I had no idea.

"Bibi, Gillian, Margot, and I were there for a while before our boyfriends came." She looked down at the thin gold band on her wedding finger. "By the time Jamie, Hudson, Win, and Brody showed up, it was dark. We drank beer and talked. That may not sound like much of an evening, but it was actually wonderful. The eight of us enjoyed discussing anything and everything. We laughed a lot together." Her eyes had a dreamy look as she reminisced. "Then someone threw down a challenge and the guys left."

"Do you know approximately what time?"

"No, I'm sorry. But it was long after midnight because I remember hearing the campanile bells faintly in the distance much earlier. Anyway, they ran off into the woods—they were having a race to the bridge—and the rest of us decided to leave. I wasn't feeling well, and Gillian took me home."

"What about Bibi and Margot?"

"Margot drove herself home. Bibi lived on the property, so she walked right up the path as usual. Later that day, we all heard Ilse was missing and we made the diner our central location, where we'd meet when we weren't out looking for her." She sat up straighter. "That was when everything changed. It was terrifying, the whole town searching for her, and the rumors circulating only added to the fear."

"What kind of rumors?"

"Oh, that she'd been abducted by a serial killer, or beamed up by aliens, or sacrificed by a cult, or eaten by bears. Someone said they saw her stumbling along the shore of the lake."

"And they didn't help her?"

"They caught a glimpse of Ilse when they were crossing the bridge, but by the time they parked the car on the little turn-off, she was gone. Or so they say."

I jotted that down.

"Were all of those theories disproven? What do you think happened?"

She shrugged. "I truly believed someone had taken her. I had nightmares for years. I still don't know what happened to her. It's unbearable. I can't imagine how difficult it is for Bibi."

"How would you describe Ilse?"

"She was a wild child."

"What do you mean by 'a wild child'?"

"Ilse did and said whatever she wanted, without regard to others. Took risks. Got into fights. It alienated a lot of people, and she didn't have many friends. We were all surprised that she'd agreed to attend something as mundane as a sleepover in the first place."

Penelope picked up a pen and began drawing on a piece of paper—looked like a meeting agenda—in front of her. I always found it interesting to peek at what people doodle and try to interpret what their subconscious may be revealing. Sometimes, it could even be a clue.

"What was the girl's name, the one who invited her over?"

"I don't know. Some junior. The police focused on that whole family but never charged them with anything. They moved away the next year—who could blame them? Never heard from them again."

She doodled faster. The image was looking like a cat, which unfortunately didn't seem like a proper clue, as far as I could tell.

"Did Ilse get into a lot of trouble?"

Penelope considered this. "Some. No one could get her to attend school regularly, or to show up anywhere she was supposed to be, so there were consequences for that. She was erratic and volatile. Her poor mother was always wringing her hands about it. Thing was, Ilse seemed to want to be with us. She'd follow us around or go to the same place we were going and sit nearby, like she was listening to everything we said. Bibi always invited her to join us, to become a member of the Larks, but Ilse refused."

"Do you think she was at the lake that night?"

Penelope added whiskers and—unexpectedly—a tiara to her cat. "I didn't see her, but she did have her hiding places. Not that I knew where any of them were, exactly. We'd see her drift by sometimes is what I mean."

"Was there any point in the evening when the women weren't together?"

"Hmm. We were generally in the same place at the bonfire, maybe in and out of the woods from time to time, but not very far from each other at any point until we went home."

Her phone made a sound, and she scanned the screen. "Are you going over to talk to Brody after this? He's checking in and, I suspect, procrastinating on starting his sculpture that he promised Bibi as a centerpiece for the party. He normally doesn't do art to order, but he lost a friendly bet with Bibi."

"Yes, I'm heading over there next."

She texted him back while I dug out one of my business cards and slid it across the desk. "If you think of anything else, would you please let me know?"

Penelope looked at it. "When do you go up for Associate Professor?"

"Next year."

"You'll be fine—look at the work you're doing! Your study of Isabella Dare is important. And let me say that I can't believe who the author turned out to be."

I smiled at her. "Me too. I never in a million years imagined that I'd meet Isabella Dare in person. And thank you for the kind words."

"Of course." She winked at me. "I'm a little jealous, you know, that you're writing about one of my best friends."

"You can too," I said. "The more, the merrier."

She laughed. "Things are as they should be. I'm winding down my career and you're beginning yours. I bet Stonedale University is thrilled with your work."

"Hardly."

"They should be. You're breaking new ground. That's very difficult to do. If you don't get tenure, it will be a travesty."

"From your lips to the tenure gods' ears." I thanked her profusely and left. There may have been a pronounced skip in my step, if only temporarily.

Following a campus map I'd printed out the night before, I found my way to the art studio, a large white space with three long tables in the center, sinks along one wall and a kiln at the far end. Brody was at the first table, staring at a good-sized lump of clay in front of him through his round wire glasses. His long hair, mostly gray with dark streaks, was pulled back into a thin ponytail that went halfway down his back. The black long-sleeved t-shirt under his blue apron was clean, but his jeans had smudges of dried clay from where he must have wiped his hands earlier.

He looked up when I greeted him. "Come in, Lila. You're right on time. Have a seat."

I settled on a stool across from him. "Thanks for seeing me. Just wanted to ask you a few questions. First of all, do you have any ideas about Gillian? Who might have wanted to hurt her, that sort of thing?"

"That's a tragedy, pure and simple. No one wanted to hurt her. She was one of the nicest people I've ever known. I've tried to imagine who could have done this, but I couldn't even give a short list of suspects. It's genuinely puzzling."

"Okay, let's switch gears a bit. What do you remember from the night Ilse disappeared?"

"Ilse Smithson? Why are we talking about that now?" He scratched his head. "Did I miss something?"

"Bibi's missing manuscript was focused on that night." I watched his face closely, but his expression didn't change. "It might be coincidence that the manuscript was stolen, but if anything in the book might be related to Gillian's death, we want to connect the dots."

"Got it." He poked at the clay with a finger. "So that particular evening was the last time we got together at home before going to college, but it was like any other night that summer. We met at the lake, we drank some beers, we goofed around."

"Did you see Ilse?"

He met my eyes. "No."

"Did the eight of you stay together all night?"

One side of his mouth went up. "People wandered around, like you do at a party. And at some point, Jamie threw down a challenge, a race to the bridge and back. It was far away and the woods were dark, but we were young and thought that sounded like a cool idea."

"What happened?"

"Jamie and I went around the left side of the lake. Hudson and Winston took the right side. Jamie was much faster than I, so it wasn't long before we were separated. Same with Hud and Win, they said."

"So in essence, you were all four separated in the forest?"

He poked at the clay harder this time, as if nudging it to take shape by itself. "I hadn't thought about it like that but yes, we were."

"When did you reunite?"

Brody's eyes seemed to flash but his voice was calm. "What are you implying, Lila?"

"I'm not implying anything. Just trying to account for everyone's movements, see how they fit together."

He nodded. "Jamie and I got back to the bonfire first. We sat on the dock with our feet in the water, talking, until Win and Hud returned."

"Who returned first?"

"Winston, but not by much."

"Then what happened?"

Brody stared at me. "Nothing. We went home."

"When did you hear about Ilse?"

"When I woke up later that morning, my father told me."

"When did you see the others again?"

He put both hands at the base of the clay and started pushing it with his thumbs. "A few hours later, at the diner."

"What did you think of their demeanors?"

His head snapped up. "We were all shocked and scared. It was clear right away that something was wrong. No one ever disappeared in Larkston."

"Is there anything else you can remember?"

"Bibi never really got over it. Changed her forever."

"What do you mean?"

"Doesn't she seem obsessed with that night to you?"

I didn't reply. If pressed, I'd have to say no. Until recently, I hadn't even known about her sister.

He returned to the clay. "Look closer."

I stopped at the gas station on the way home to fill up the tank. The brightly lit building was oddly comforting, taking the edge off of the gloom that had been generated by Brody's disconcerting last words.

Or maybe it was the proximity to caffeine.

At the beverage station, I ran into Detective Ortiz, who was pouring cream into a large coffee. Reaching out for the pot of hazelnut, I casually asked how the investigation was going.

"Fine, thank you." He jabbed the wooden stirrer into the liquid and spun it around.

I finished pouring and set the pot back on the burner. "Any leads?"

He took a long sip.

I'd been down this road before, trying to elicit information from the police, so I set up the old I Share, You Share play. "I know about the missing manuscript. From Bibi's house. Where Gillian was found."

The detective remained silent as he pressed a lid onto his cup.

"Do you think it has anything to do with—"

He narrowed his eyes. "We're not going to talk about this, Dr. Maclean. I know about how you've offered help on occasion to the Stonedale PD."

"If by 'offered help,' you mean *solved* cases—"

"But here in Larkston, we would greatly appreciate it if you'd let us do our job. And please keep the facts of the case to yourself. For example, we would strongly prefer that information about the manuscript be kept quiet for now. It's evidence that doesn't need to be circulating yet...if ever."

I snapped a lid onto my own cup. The air between us felt charged. No sense in antagonizing him any further at this point.

"Of course, Detective. I completely understand."

He lifted his coffee as if toasting me for having responded correctly.

As I toasted him back, my phone lit up with a text from Bibi.

It was three exclamation points with a link. I clicked it and was taken to a new post from the *Larkston Live* site: "Mysterious Manuscript Stolen!"

Chapter 10

The brief article had only stated that a new lead in the Gillian Shane case involved the theft of a manuscript from the crime scene. It hadn't said anything about who had written it or what it was about. Back at Callahan House, I looked for Bibi and found her in the garage cutting a small wooden shape with a jigsaw.

I waited until she was finished and asked how Tacey could have known about the manuscript.

"Someone must have talked to Tacey. Maybe someone at the police department." She set down the saw and unplugged it.

"Not a Lark? Or a husband of a Lark?"

"They would never," Bibi said emphatically.

"Is there anything we can do?"

"No. And while it isn't great that everyone knows the book exists, at least Tacey doesn't have her hands on it. She'd be serving up scandalous morsels piping hot to the whole town otherwise."

"What's in the manuscript that would be considered scandalous?"

She brushed sawdust from her work apron, but it clung to her flannel shirt. "For starters, remember that this all happened decades ago. Times were different. There were certainly folks in this town who would think eight high school seniors staying out most of the night would verge on disgraceful, especially since we were four couples. Some of that kind of thinking has never really left

Larkston. We still have our morality monitors."

"And Tacey would be one of those?" I guessed.

"Definitely."

"But not everyone would think that..."

"No. But there was an incidence of skinny dipping," she said with a twinkle in her eye. "Which I may have mentioned."

I waved that away. "Also not terribly scandalous."

Bibi loosened the vice holding the wood and held it up for examination, then added it to a shelf where several other pieces of the same size were already stacked.

"What are you making?"

"Partridges to hang out front before the party. We have pines, not pear trees, but hopefully no one will complain."

"Adorable." I marveled at her creativity.

She removed her safety glasses and leaned against the workbench, crossing her arms. "On a more serious note, I did write about a long-time feud between Margot and Gillian. I wish I hadn't put their secret on paper."

"What were they fighting about?"

"Hudson. Margot had a crush on him. They were extremely flirty, and Gillian didn't like it. Can't say I blame her."

"Ah."

"But Margot was destined to be with Win. They were from the two richest families in town, aside from the miners."

"The what now?"

Bibi smiled. "Oh, Jamie and Hudson used to call themselves that: the miners. The original Callahans were silver miners, though the family retired from that business ages ago, and the Shanes were rock miners. They still own the old town quarry, in fact, though it has long since flooded."

"Got it."

"Margot and Win's parents had paired them off at birth,

practically. They were a golden couple: he was the quarterback and the class president, and she was head cheerleader and vice president. They were homecoming king and queen several years running as well. You know the type."

"Yes. What did Winston think about Margot's feelings for Hudson?"

"I don't think he ever noticed. He's surrounded by a thick cloud of his own importance. He can barely remember anyone's name if he hasn't already known them his whole life. But Gillian definitely noticed."

That was interesting. "What did she do?"

"Confronted her. That night, actually, she caught Margot and Hudson in an embrace in the woods. Right before the guys ran off. I'd forgotten about that," she said softly. "Margot swore it was the only time they kissed and that it meant nothing, but Gillian was always distrustful of her after that."

"Did Brody have any issues with anyone?" I asked, remembering how he bristled when I pushed for details about the bridge race.

"Pen thought he was cheating on her with Margot. They got into a fight that night as well. He was angry that she accused him of that, especially once we realized soon afterwards that it was Hudson who was involved with Margot."

"Did you write about that?"

"Yes. I wrote about everything that happened. I shouldn't have." She looked thoughtful. "Now that you've spoken to everyone there that night, what do you think?"

"It sounds like a typical night, for the most part. As you've said, primarily high school drama." There was something at the back of my mind, some tickle of an idea, but I couldn't seem to pull it forward. "I'm curious...what was the conclusion you drew in the book?"

Bibi looked down. "I'm sorry, but I don't want to say any more about the book. Particularly right now."

Why wouldn't she tell me?

Was she trying to hide something about her friends?

Or herself?

I was in the parlor working on my laptop, frantically trying to pull together my notes for the looming presentation, when there was a knock on the front door.

When I peeked through the sidelight and saw who was standing on the porch, I sighed. It was tempting to pretend no one was home, but I forced myself to open the heavy door and display a smile.

"Hello, Dr. Maclean," said the tall man in a long wool coat. "I'd heard you were here."

I greeted the most influential person at my university, trying to process his presence. "Please come in."

Chancellor Trawley Wellington strode forward, pulling off a black leather glove. "I'm here to see Professor Callahan. Is she available?"

"I'm afraid she's resting. Is there anything I can help you with instead?"

"Could you give me a tour?" He turned his head from side to side, perhaps cataloging the furnishings that were reflected in his wireless glasses.

I stared at him.

"It's been awhile since I've been to Callahan House. I heard it was up for sale, and I would like to make an offer. It would be an excellent space for Stonedale University retreats and functions."

Bibi had just made her announcement last night. "How did you—"

"My wife Patsy is from Larkston. She remains well-connected and, accordingly, hears all kinds of things."

"I see." All I knew about the chancellor's wife was that she was a gracious hostess fond of costume parties—I'd even seen her dressed as a mermaid once to accompany the chancellor's own captain get-up.

"Patsy and I met at Callahan College and attended a number of events here together during that time."

"I didn't know that you attended—"

"*Before* I went to Harvard, of course."

"Of course." He had a reputation for working that fact into as many conversations as he could.

The chancellor tapped his foot. Literally.

"As I said, Bibi is not available right now." I smiled at him. "Would you like me to have her call you?"

He produced a business card seemingly from thin air and extended it toward me. "Are there any other offers?"

"It's not even on the market yet, so—"

"Good." He pulled his gloves on. "I'm sure everyone at Stonedale University would be very disappointed if you were unable to persuade Professor Callahan to accept our offer."

It was suddenly hard to breathe.

He turned to leave, tossing a comment over his shoulder first. "I trust that your sabbatical has been productive. You're going up for tenure next year, yes?"

Downright chilling, that.

Later, I hurried through the snowflakes toward the student union for my presentation, trying not to slip on the ice. I pushed my speed as much as I dared until someone stepped out from behind one of the colorfully beribboned pine trees, right in front of me. I drew back with such haste that I would have fallen if the person hadn't clutched my arms and wrenched me back upright. Once I caught my breath, I realized that Tacey Throckham was the mountain with whom I had collided.

"I need to talk to you," she said, squeezing my hands.

"What is *happening* right now?" I pulled away from her.

"I'm sorry, but this is urgent. You're close to Bibi, right?"

"I'm staying with her, if that's what you mean."

"I meant 'close' as in friend, but proximity works too. I have a message for you. Pay attention." She snapped her fingers in my face. "Someone called me and said that if I didn't stop talking about Ilse Smithson, I'd be sorry."

"What? Who?"

"I don't know. The number was blocked. It was distorted, like someone was trying to disguise their voice."

"Why did you answer a blocked number?"

"I answer everything." She sniffed. "I have an obligation to take all tips from my devoted readers."

"Male or female?"

"I really couldn't say. We're getting off track here, I think. I'm only saying this because you better be careful. I've heard that you and Bibi are asking questions about Ilse too."

"How did you hear that?"

She gave me an oh-please look. "This is a small town, Lila. Word travels fast. Especially when you have a tip line, like I do. News comes rolling in at all hours of the day and night."

Either we'd been overheard, or one of Bibi's friends was the source of the information, which was disturbing, at best.

A few hours later, I'd made it through my presentation. The room was much more crowded than I'd anticipated, and I'd enjoyed the lively question-and-answer period, including a moment where I'd had to dance around the issue a bit to avoid revealing Isabella Dare's true identity. I respected Bibi's wishes, but I hoped she would claim her name before too long. I didn't want to slip up in public and it was becoming more difficult. I had to work extremely hard not to look directly at her during the talk.

Penelope came over to thank me profusely for putting the talk together on such short notice, and I thanked her in turn for inviting me. As I packed up my notes, Bibi gave me a quick hug, saying she was proud of me, had enjoyed herself tremendously, and she would see me at Callahan House later.

"Lila!" A familiar voice cut through the din. My cousin and colleague Calista James waved at me from the back of the room.

I wished Penelope and Bibi a good night and went over to Calista, who was buttoning up her wine-colored wool coat.

"You were fabulous," she said, hugging me. "I bet everybody in town will want to read your Dare book when it comes out now."

I laughed. "You are extraordinarily nice and an excellent liar."

"Can you go for a drink and catch up?" She added a black beret atop her platinum blonde bob and adjusted it to the perfect angle. "We haven't seen each other in weeks. I need a cousin fix."

I glanced at my watch. "Absolutely. And I need a cousin fix too."

"Nate's here as well," she said, referring to one of our best friends. "He got a call, so he said he'd meet us outside. What's happening with you two, anyway?"

She was under the impression that Nate Clayton and I were soulmates and was forever hoping to catch a glimpse of romantic evidence to prove her point. But I'd been dating Lex for years, and Nate wandered in and out of a relationship with a brilliant professor up in Fort Collins. So her hopes were continually dashed.

"Nothing, same as every time you ask." I looped my bag over

my shoulder and gestured toward the door. "You're going to have to give up on us sooner or later."

"Never." She tucked her my arm into mine and we began walking.

I smiled at her fondly and changed the subject to her boyfriend Francisco, our resident academic superstar. Ever since his first book on the infamous Damon von Tussel had gone mainstream, he'd been in high demand as a speaker. His latest book on Flynn McMaster, another author who was no stranger to controversy, was causing a stir already.

"He's home, finishing his book. It's due soon. He sends his love, though." We followed the last of the crowd into the hallway and down the stairs.

"Give him my love back, along with best wishes for triumphant crossing of the finish line. How's he doing?"

"Oh, stressed beyond belief. Like every academic we know."

"Amen to that."

My phone alert sounded. Tacey had posted a new item on her site: "Chancellor Craves Callahan House!"

What the heck? I knew I hadn't mentioned it to her. I scanned the text, which claimed that the chancellor was planning to acquire the mansion.

The only people who knew about his offer were the chancellor himself, Bibi, and me. Why would Bibi or the chancellor give Tacey the tip?

Then I remembered his wife Patsy was from Larkston.

Mystery solved, probably.

You'd think that Tacey could wait until there was an actual deal before announcing things. Or maybe she wanted to be the first person to break the story. I thought there were guidelines about that, confirmation procedures for journalists, though social media did have a way of blurring gossip and legitimate news, and if her site was now a blog instead of a paper, well, I didn't know what the rules were about that.

When we reached the bottom of the stairs, I felt a tug on my arm. "What's it going to take to get you back to Stonedale? We miss you."

"Nate!" I took in his tousled caramel-colored hair and crooked grin and realized how much I'd missed him too.

He swept me into a bear hug, smelling, as always, of soap. "Great job tonight. No matter how many times I hear you talk about Isabella Dare, I never get bored."

"That's one of the reasons I like you so much," I said, smiling at him.

"I knew it had to be something like that." He zipped up his gray fleece jacket. "Let's go toast you."

We dashed through the snow to our cars and successfully moved our reunion to the nearby Larkston Inn. We ordered their specialty "winter chaser"—a tasty blend of cocoa, coffee, and butterscotch schnapps—off of the chalkboard menu. At first sip, I proclaimed it my new favorite beverage, in the Drinks That Arrive In Mugs category. Nate challenged it with a late Peak House Ale entry, but Calista ultimately pronounced that there was room for everyone on the podium, given that hot and cold drinks deserved separate consideration, which made us all happy. She always proved to be a fair judge in such deliberations.

The dining area was charming, with large comfortable booths and Tiffany-style lights overhead. It was dark enough in the room to feel like a special night out yet quiet enough to hear each other speak. We caught up on campus news and exchanged progress reports on our respective research projects.

"And how's it going with tenure?" I asked Nate. He'd submitted the formal dossier not long ago.

"Made it through the department so far," he said.

"I'm sure the review went well. No surprises?"

He made a face. "A little birdie told me that a certain *someone* did attempt the obstruction play that he's so fond of—you know, raising capricious questions about the candidate's publications and whatnot—but the rest of the committee was familiar enough with his trickeries that he didn't gain much traction."

"Are you talking about Norton?" Our colleague, Professor Smythe, had a long history of attempting to throw a wrench into every tenure bid, primarily to feed his highly inflated sense of superiority. He saw himself as a gatekeeper of the first degree, even though he had long ago—whether he realized it or not—lost the respect of most faculty members through his habit of condescending to one and all.

"Who else?" He drummed the table.

Calista bent her head toward him, setting her hammered gold earrings swinging. "What little birdie was it?"

"That I will never tell. As you know, deliberations are confidential."

"They're supposed to be," she replied, "yet things *do* manage to get out, don't they?"

"Well, congratulations," I said to Nate. "You've made it through the first hurdle. This round of drinks is on me, and when you get tenure, I'll buy you a whole bottle and then some. By the way, I admire how calm you are about the whole thing. I'll probably be a mess for months on end."

He grimaced. "Trying to keep a brave face, but this process is emotionally grueling. I'm doing positive visualizations...and daily affirmations...heck, if I had one, I'd be wearing a good luck charm around my neck every day until the trustees finalize the process, if that would help."

I looked deeply into his bright blue eyes. "You *are* going to get tenure. You deserve it. And we will plan an enormous bash to celebrate you and your accomplishment."

"Seriously appreciate the support." Nate smiled, his teeth very white next to his ruddy cheeks. He maintained a sunburn year round, which wasn't hard to do when you spent the majority of time outdoors climbing, skiing, and hiking. I'd thought, more than once, how much it suited him.

"Now," he said, "may I turn our attention to the elephant in the room?"

"What elephant?" I asked.

He lowered his voice. "Is it true that Bibi is Isabella Dare?"

"How did you hear that?"

"Aunt Vi told me," Calista admitted, unwinding her lavender scarf and setting it down next to her. "She didn't mean to, but she was going on and on about how kind Isabella was to offer you a sabbatical space. Once she realized that she'd said Isabella instead of Bibi, she begged me not to tell anyone."

Calista was more like a sister than a cousin—she'd lived with us after her parents died—and I wasn't surprised that my mother assumed she knew. It had been extremely hard not to tell my cousin that Bibi was Isabella, but I'd honored my host's request. The only reason my mother knew was because Bibi had said at the conference that she knew my mother; I had to make sure that the person with whom I'd be living for a semester was in fact who she said she was, so we had a long conversation about Bibi Callahan and in the middle of that, my mother made the connection. She—and Calista—had always maintained that our family had psychic abilities; sometimes she backed up that claim by knowing things she had no way of knowing. We all did. It didn't happen often enough to put out a shingle and offer readings, but it was a thing we had learned to accept.

"Ah. But how did *you* know, Nate?"

"I walked into Calista's office at the exact moment she freaked out about what your mother said—"

"I was not freaking out!" She swatted him with scarf fringe.

"There were gasps and shrieks. Then she immediately administered a blood vow demanding silence. See the scar?" He held up his palm.

Calista shook her head at him, then touched my hand lightly. "We haven't talked much about Gillian Shane. How are you doing?"

"Everyone is devastated."

"Do the police have any leads?" Nate took another drink, then gazed into the liquid concoction as if trying to fathom its secrets.

I took another sip as well. It was indeed delicious.

"If so, they haven't told us. There is one thing, though. The same night that Gillian was killed, a manuscript was stolen."

Calista leaned forward. "A manuscript? What kind of manuscript?"

"The first Athena Bolt book Bibi ever wrote. Unpublished. She never submitted it for publication. I actually found it in a desk drawer when I was organizing her study. She'd forgotten about it, she said."

"Oh, Lila, that's an enormous discovery." Her gray eyes lit up.

"Well, right now, it's missing. And it was the only copy." I paused. "It has been widely reported that the manuscript is missing, but they haven't identified Bibi as the author yet. You have to promise me that you'll keep that—all of this conversation—to yourselves."

"We always do," Calista said. "You don't even have to say that."

"It makes me feel better to invoke the cone of silence," I said. "To be sure we're all on the same page."

"Going in the vault per usual," Nate said smoothly. "Please continue."

"Bibi and I think Gillian had the manuscript with her when she was attacked. The killer may not have known what it was...or perhaps they killed to get it."

"Could someone have stolen it earlier?" Nate asked. "Before Gillian was attacked?"

"Not easily. It was in a locked drawer."

Calista looked confused. "If it was in a locked drawer, how did Gillian get ahold of it?"

Heat rose to my face. "I gave her the key."

Nate whistled.

"Not so that she could get the manuscript. I thought she was returning the key to Bibi along with the tea we'd made, but she delivered the tea and went into the study instead. Gillian was a literary agent, and Bibi thinks she was curious about the content."

"How did she even know about the manuscript in the first place?" Nate asked.

"During the book club meeting, I mentioned that four Isabella Dare books existed, not just the three already published."

"Oh no," Calista said.

"Exactly. It was my fault."

"No, it wasn't," Nate said. "You didn't kill her."

"Then why do I feel so awful about it?"

"All you did was give someone a key," he said. "You didn't know what would come of it."

I thought back to my conversation in the kitchen with Gillian and something dawned on me. "Technically, *she* picked up the key from the counter and insisted that she be the one to deliver it to Bibi."

Calista nodded emphatically. "See? You didn't even give it to her in the first place. And you certainly didn't know that she wouldn't immediately give it to Bibi."

"Or sneak into the study to look at something that didn't belong to her," Nate added. "She did that all by herself."

I gratefully processed their take on the situation.

Calista traced her finger around the rim of the mug. "What's the manuscript about, anyway?"

"It's fictionalized, but Bibi centered the book on the night that her younger sister disappeared." I gave them all the details I'd learned. "What makes everything even more ominous is the fact that every guest present when Gillian died was also at Callahan House the night Ilse went missing."

"That's quite a correlation," Nate said.

"Bibi asked me to help sort through potentials, and I've spoken to each of her guests. But they all seem very nice and not in any way..."

"Murder-y?" Calista suggested.

"Exactly."

The campus bells were chiming midnight as we walked down the street toward our cars. The moonlight shimmered off of the snow around us, turning everything silver as if we were trapped in a world made of ice.

I shivered and pulled my coat closer. All I wanted to do was get back to my cozy little cottage and collapse. The storefronts were dark, and I was glad not to be alone—even in a small town like Larkston, things could be waiting in the night. As we passed the alley between a flower shop and the *Larkston Live* office, I saw a lump in the center of the yawning gap.

"What's that?" I asked Nate and Calista, pointing.

We turned and went closer.

Then I wished we hadn't.

Chapter 11

Tacey Throckham was dead. As was the case with Gillian, her scarf appeared to be the murder weapon. Officers arrived soon after we called; the red-and-blue lights sliding over the buildings added another confusing visual layer to the already surreal landscape. We spoke with them individually, then regrouped in front of the flower shop.

"What happens now?" Calista asked. She rubbed one of her eyes.

Nate yawned. "No idea."

We were all exhausted. I went over to Detective Ortiz, who eyed me warily, probably expecting me to launch into yet another attempt to ascertain the official perspective on the event. He'd been focused on efficiency first and foremost, marching us rapidly through the statement process, and he'd made it clear that information was only going to be flowing in one direction no matter what. Even when I'd told him about Tacey's mysterious phone caller, which I thought was particularly relevant, he had accepted the story without remark and refused to discuss it further.

"Do you need anything else from us?" I asked quietly.

"You're all free to go." He moved closer to the group and handed around business cards. "If you remember anything at all that might be useful, call us."

He left us to our goodbyes, which we said somberly.

Poor Tacey.

* * *

That night, I dreamt of Callahan House. First, I was in the study on the carpet, trying to elude the wispy gray tentacles that uncoiled themselves from all four walls, reaching for me. After I awoke in a panic and calmed myself down, I drifted off again to find myself looking at Silver Rush Lake through the trees. A group of people were huddled around the bonfire, whispering. I crept closer trying to hear. Their words ran together in a silky web of sound. As I strained to make sense of what they were saying, they turned toward the water, which had begun to churn. Something was coming toward us. I felt their fear and wanted to back away, but my feet wouldn't move.

A chime startled me awake; it was a text from Bibi inviting me to join her for breakfast in the dining room. I lay in the bed for a moment before throwing back the covers, waiting for the uneasiness that lingered over me to dissipate. Then I dressed and went over to the house, where she was already at the table.

"Good morning. I've made oatmeal and we have fresh fruit—is there anything else you'd like?"

"That sounds great, thank you." I joined her, grabbing the mug of coffee she'd poured for me and practically shotgunning it.

Bibi paused, a spoon halfway to her mouth, and measured me with a look. "How are you today, Lila?"

I forced myself to slow down, pour some cream into my coffee, and stir it. Like a person who has shared a meal with other humans before.

She went on. "I heard about Tacey—I'm sorry you and your friends were the ones to find her. It must have been appalling."

"It was—and sad, of course. She was just lying there in the dark, all alone."

"Is it true that she was strangled, like Gillian?"

"Yes." An image of the scarf twisted around her neck flashed before me. I turned my head and closed my eyes for a second.

Bibi waited until I opened them, then passed me a bowl of fruit. "Eat something, dear. It will make you feel better."

"Thanks." I spooned some strawberries into my oatmeal. After a few bites, I was steadier.

"Do you—or the police—think it's related?"

"I do, but they didn't say anything one way or another."

"I'm sure you pressed them on it."

"I tried." I thought about how different things had been with Lex, how much I'd taken for granted his willingness to allow certain things to be known. He'd always drawn a careful line between what he could and could not tell me, officially, but at least he allowed me to express theories and make connections. He would validate the ones he thought were worth pursuing.

Detective Ortiz acted like I was a stranger with no business thinking about anything related to the murders.

Which I guess could be one way of looking at it.

"Let's draw upon *our* professional expertise, shall we?" Bibi smiled. "We are both devoted readers and writers of mystery, after all. Not that I'm making a game of guessing what happened to people we knew. No, I mean it more as an academic exercise, a compiling of literary examples."

I agreed and joined her in making a list of stories that might shed light upon the current situation. It served, paradoxically, as a potent distraction from the matters at hand, but we didn't generate anything that could power a lightbulb moment.

Once the coffee pot had run dry, Bibi sighed. "I can't help but feel like we're missing something that's right in front of us."

"That's how I feel most of the time, actually."

"How frustrating. I'm sure the police also suspect an association between the two crimes, but I don't know how well the investigators knew the women. On the other hand, I knew them *both* very well. It seems as though I should be able to establish a clear link, but I'm coming up blank."

"Not for a lack of trying," I consoled her.

"Perhaps I need to find another angle."

"Well, let's consider their relationship. How did Gillian feel about Tacey?"

"I don't think she had any feelings toward her, other than as a former classmate. Gillian and Tacey didn't travel in the same circles."

"Gillian was in your circle."

"Of course."

"Who was in Tacey's?"

Bibi put her elbows on the table, laced her fingers together, and rested her chin on them. "I don't know if she had many friends. She regularly reminded most of us that her position as a reporter meant she had to be a 'neutral party'—her words. Which was highly ironic given how biased we all thought she was, constructing stories that were more faithful to her own desires and opinions than to any objective sense of truth. I liked her well enough, and she felt kindly enough toward me to come to the winter party, though that may have been to gather fodder for news stories, now that I think about it."

The doorbell rang out three sonorous tones, the last melancholy note hanging in the air for a beat afterwards.

Our eyes met.

"Are you expecting anyone?" I asked. "I haven't had a chance to tell you that before the presentation last night, Tacey came up to me and said someone had warned her not to talk about Ilse anymore. She suggested we should take heed as well."

"Well that's sobering. Was Tacey upset?"

"She didn't seem particularly worried—said that such things

went with the territory—but thought *we* might want to be careful."

"And I agree, so I'll look through the window before opening the door."

She rose and went through the parlor. I brushed the crumbs from my lap and carried the breakfast dishes over to the counter.

"It's Margot," she called, relief in her voice.

I walked down the hallway as Margot came into the foyer. She was holding a large white bag. "Hello to you both," she said. "Win and I are on the way home from church and had some extra doughnuts. Less of a crowd than usual—I think because of the snow." She looked over her shoulder. "He's in the car on the phone."

"That's so kind of you." Bibi accepted the bag and offered her a drink.

"Oh no, thanks. I've had three cups of tea already, trying to stay warm."

"Come inside and sit by the fire for a minute."

"I'd love to." Margot waved at the idling black Rolls Royce and shrugged off her coat, which she hung up in the large closet behind the door. As she settled in one of the chairs by the fireplace, I heard a door slam outside. Winston appeared on the threshold shortly afterwards.

Bibi greeted him and repeated her offer. He too, declined.

"Hello, ladies." He kept his coat on, tucking it carefully around him as he sat in the chair opposite Margot's. "How are you doing today?"

"We've been discussing what happened to Tacey," Bibi said quietly.

"It's a *terrible* thing, two murders within weeks of each other. I don't know what this town is coming to." Winston frowned.

"It is terrible," Margot echoed. "If I'd known the other day was the last time we'd see Tacey alive, I wouldn't have been so beastly. I feel awful."

"You were protecting me," Bibi consoled her.

"I know, but I didn't have to lose my temper like that."

"Keeping your temper is not your strong point, my friend." Bibi smiled at her.

"True enough." Margot crossed one leg over the other. "I'm not proud of that, by the way."

"But it has served you well." Bibi turned to me. "Margot was already famous as a model in New York when I was going to graduate school there. Whenever we went out in public, fans surrounded her. She had to make her voice heard often in order to claim some space for herself to exist in the world, to do normal things that the rest of us took for granted."

"That's not an issue anymore, though. Now that I'm older. Which is both a blessing and a curse." Margot smoothed her hair back.

Winston coughed. "You're still the most gorgeous woman I've ever seen."

"Thank you, my love. Though I no longer care about any of that. We are each and every one of us so more than what we look like, after all."

Bibi and I smiled at each other. Margot's words and attitude were not quite matching up, but neither of us was going to call her out on it. Plus, she had a point: we *were* all far more than what we looked like.

"Anyway," Margot continued, "speaking of Tacey, Win and I saw the item in *Larkston Live* about the chancellor of Stonedale having some interest in purchasing Callahan House. Is it true?"

"Yes. He made me an offer yesterday. Apparently, he stopped by while I was resting and Lila spoke with him, then he emailed me afterwards."

Margot regarded me with interest. "You teach at Stonedale,

don't you, Lila? What do you think of good old Trawley?"

I chose my words carefully. "He's energetic."

Margot emitted a throaty laugh. "Very democratic. I take it from your answer that you're not a fan?"

With my luck, they were all best friends and whatever I said was going straight from my mouth to his ears. As I wrestled with my response, I could feel my face turning bright red. Curse you, traitorous skin!

Winston chuckled and addressed Margot. "Don't put her on the spot like that." To me, he added, "We attended Callahan together."

"Did everyone in town go to Callahan College?"

"Not *everyone*," Margot drew herself up. "It's exclusive. Quite difficult to get into. Known as a bit of a feeder for the Ivies, if people were continuing to graduate school. And Callahan has students from all around the world wanting to attend."

Winston waved his hand languidly. "And Tarpley—"

"It's Trawley," Margot interjected.

"—later went to Harvard," Winston said. "As he's probably told you countless times, I'm sure." His eyebrows remained stationed high in question mode until I acknowledged his point.

"But everyone in *our* group did go to Callahan," Bibi confirmed. "There were perks to being friends with Jamie, we learned over time. He had a kind soul, and his family had connections at the college, which was named after them to honor the role they played in its foundation as well as their generous support over the years. I know he asked his parents to help us out, and whatever they did worked because we all were offered scholarships."

That also explained, probably, why several of the group members had been hired at Callahan College later.

"In any case," Winston said, "our friend Trapley—"

"Trawley," Margot corrected him.

"—always viewed me as a rival. He never quite forgave me for winning student body president in college. He really wanted that."

I was having a strong case of *déjà vu*, flashing back to the conversation in Winston's office about his competition with Hudson. Clearly, Winston liked to compete with people, even if he didn't recognize it himself. Some people were like that.

He forged onward. "When we both rose to leadership roles at our respective schools, his competitive streak grew even more overt. Now it wasn't just Trappy versus me—"

"*Trawley*," Margot said again, slightly louder.

"—it was Stonedale versus Callahan. He regularly sends me emails crowing about achievements, hires, and rankings, even sports victories."

His expression turned crafty. "In fact, if you are ever interested in a position with our English department, please give me a call, Layla."

"*Lila*." Margot smiled apologetically at me.

I thanked him and filed that away for future reference.

You never know.

"Winston, my love, you're drifting." Margot shot him a pointed look.

"Right. Well, we sure would like to throw our hats into the ring, Bibi. Through the generosity of the Callahan family, we've hosted college events on this property for years. We are connected through tradition, and we'd like to continue that. If you're going to sell to anyone, please sell it to us."

Bibi looked at him for a long time. "I didn't know about the situation with you and Trawley. Once Callahan House goes on the market, after the holidays, we can talk. Thank you for your interest."

"Fair enough. Thank you, Bibi." He stood and moved to the

door.

Margot gave Bibi a dazzling smile. "One other thing: would you ever consider bequeathing your papers to the college? Anything related to your books and so forth. We are extremely interested in compiling more works by Larkston authors and scholars for the college library. It's a new alumni group initiative, something to celebrate our alums and community members in a special collection. The librarians would have the final say, of course, as the official curators, but they are excited about the possibilities. I am starting to reach out to esteemed candidates. Like yourself."

Bibi laughed. "Certainly my files would have no value."

"Actually, Bibi," I said slowly, "future Isabella Dare scholars would probably love to get their hands on them. I can't tell you how much it's helped me to be able to see the materials."

Margot focused a laser-beam of hope in Bibi's direction. My host said she would think about it. There was still the matter of a pseudonym to consider, if she was able to hold onto it during the investigation into Gillian's death. Margot wisely took this in stride, promised to come up with potential privacy strategies if Bibi decided to go forward, and followed her husband out the door.

"Whew," Bibi said. "The vultures are circling. I don't mean anything negative toward Win and Margot. They're my dear friends. But to me, this is an emotional thing—the end of an era—and they're a little too ready to pounce. All I did was mention that I might be putting the place on the market and we instantly have two potential offers."

"Not a bad problem to have."

"True. But, ugh, sparring administrators. I don't want to be at the center of any lifelong duels."

"It could be fun, and it could raise the price quite a bit," I said.

"That's true," she agreed. "About the price, anyway."

Then I remembered, with a jolt, the chancellor's comment as

he walked out the door. I didn't genuinely think he would allow a failed real estate deal to have any bearing on my tenure application, but what if he did?

Perhaps I needed to avoid urging on any additional president-vs.-chancellor skirmish scenarios.

Chapter 12

I spent the rest of Sunday re-reading my mystery draft. It was as finished as I knew how to make it, and Bibi was right: the next step was to show someone. As I printed out the pages, I watched the snow falling onto the green branches outside my window. The storm they'd been promising all week was amping up. If it stuck, we'd have a white Christmas, which was not always the case in Colorado.

Once the novel was done printing, I inserted it into a three-ring notebook that I packed in my satchel alongside my laptop and my critical study on Isabella Dare. It was hard to believe there were two book manuscripts in my bag, when not so long ago, even *one* had once seemed absolutely impossible. I didn't know what would happen in the future, if either one would ever be published, but at least I had written them.

Just then, the furnace in the hallway closet made an odd clicking sound, then a louder scraping sound, then a horrible grinding sound. By the time I had crossed the room and thrown open the door, it had gone silent. I inspected it, which led to zero discoveries since I knew nothing about furnaces other than the fact that you had to change the filters. I stared in dismay, then closed the door.

Great. Bibi had lent me her cottage and I had broken it.

I called her to explain what had happened. Ten minutes later,

Bibi was at the door in coveralls with a red metal toolbox in one hand and a headlamp on her forehead.

"Let's have a look-see," she said briskly.

I stepped backward to let her into the cottage. "I'm sorry, Bibi. I know it's going to be expensive. I'd be happy to contribute toward the cost of repair or replacement."

"You will do no such thing. And if it is broken, no worries. It was an old furnace and a matter of time. We replaced the whole heating system in the other cottage last year. This one has lasted longer than we ever thought it would."

Bibi went over to the furnace, removed the front panel, and peered into the machinery. Then she unlatched the toolbox and turned on her headlamp. Confidently, she fished out various tools, wires, and metal objects that I didn't recognize and applied them to the furnace in mysterious ways. Before too long, the furnace was practically purring.

I applauded. It seemed like the correct response.

Bibi looked up and laughed. "That may be premature. I'm not sure how long this will hold."

"I won't ask what specifically was broken because it wouldn't make sense to me anyhow, but, for the record, I'm extremely impressed."

"Don't be. I think we'll still need to replace this eventually, but perhaps we can coax it to limp into the new year." She replaced the items in her toolbox and wiped her hand on a rag that she pulled out of her pocket.

"Where did you learn how to do…" I gestured toward the furnace, "*that*?"

Bibi laughed. "Since retiring, I've taken all sorts of classes. Painting, cooking, and home repair. Whatever strikes my fancy. I enjoy learning new things."

"I do too. Especially when it involves reading. There is nothing like being plunged into unexpected action, thrilled by a beautiful sentence, or confronted by a new idea that changes your understanding of the world."

"I absolutely agree. Reading is one of life's greatest joys."

We smiled at each other.

"I was about to adjourn to the library to start a brand new mystery, in fact. Would you care to join me for some reading time?"

I eagerly agreed, locked up the cottage, and followed her to the main house. She swapped out the coveralls for a lumpy woolen sweater and made some tea. We had barely settled in with our books when the doorbell cut into the silence, momentarily dampening the mood. There was something about those particular three notes that evoked sadness. I wondered why anyone would have chosen them to announce guests, especially since the tone was so at odds with the bright and cheerful exterior of Callahan House.

Bibi set down her cup and walked to the door. I trailed behind her, still on edge from Tacey's warning.

A woman approximately the same height as Bibi stood on the front step. She was wrapped in a camel-colored coat and held a tapestry bag. I relaxed slightly.

"Hello," Bibi said, a slight question in her tone.

"I'm looking for Bibi Callahan." From behind her, a wind gust blasted snow into the foyer.

"You found me," Bibi said, stepping back. "Please come in."

The woman moved forward. Once Bibi had closed the door, she smiled at her. "Thanks. Cold out there."

"How may I help you?" Bibi asked politely, brushing snow from her sleeve.

"I'm sorry," said the woman, gripping her bag tightly in both hands. "I won't take more than a minute of your time, but could we please sit down?"

Bibi didn't even hesitate, leading her guest immediately over to the fireplace. Once we were all seated, she looked expectantly at the woman.

She set the bag down next to her chair. “There’s no easy way to say this.”

“Please speak freely,” Bibi encouraged her. “You have nothing to fear.”

“I have some news about your sister.”

“Go on.” Bibi’s tone cooled.

She put both hands up to her chest. “I’m her. I’m Ilse.”

Bibi didn’t move for a long moment. Her eyes wide, she examined the visitor from head to toe. “How could this be?”

“It’s true. I’ll prove it.” The visitor pulled up her right sleeve and showed Bibi something on the inside of her wrist—a small symbol I couldn’t quite make out.

Bibi stared at it, then slid off the sofa and opened her arms to the visitor. They hugged for a long time, crying and exclaiming and talking over one another. I slipped from the room, wanting to give them some privacy.

After I closed the door behind me, I turned around and jumped at the sight of Alice looming so closely that I couldn’t move in either direction.

Her mouth was opening slowly. Pinned against the door, I watched her teeth come closer to my face. I was mesmerized and horrified all at once.

Finally, her high, clear voice formed words: “She’s here!” She giggled and repeated it over and over as she lurched away.

I sagged against the wall in relief.

I didn’t *really* think she was going to bite me.

Not for more than a moment, anyway.

By the time I opened my eyes the next day, it was mid-morning, but a quick glance out the window showed that it was still dark gray outside. I showered, dressed in warm layers, and went over to the main house.

Bibi was in the parlor with Ilse. When I walked in and they looked up to say hello, I was struck by the resemblance—both had long white braids, both had green eyes, and both were knitting at the same speed. The latter didn't count as familial, but it deepened the impression that they looked so alike, they could be twins.

"Lila! Meet Ilse." Bibi was glowing. "Sorry I didn't introduce you properly last night, but I was well and truly speechless."

Ilse aimed a smile at me, then back at Bibi. "I can hardly believe I'm here."

I sank onto the sofa. "When was the last time you were in town?" I didn't know how else to frame it. *Where did you come from?* sounded rude, somehow.

"Bibi said you know the story. That's the last time I was here." She yanked some yarn out of her tapestry bag. "I've been in California. With Jensen."

"Jamie's older brother," Bibi said to me. "The one who went away before we graduated from high school."

"I know there was a lot of confusion about my leaving," Ilse said slowly. "But we ran away together that night I supposedly went missing. It's that simple."

"He left earlier, though," Bibi said, still clearly confused.

"He came back for me. We'd been in touch. We had made plans."

"Why didn't you let us know you were alive, at least?" Bibi said sadly. "So many of us have worried about you for years."

"I promised Jensen." She shrugged. "That was his one request. I was so in love that I would have done anything he asked. Anything. And you know he had that awful break with his parents. He made it on his own, though. He's a very successful businessman.

Or..." her face fell. "He *was*. He died. Now I'm a widow."

Bibi and I both expressed our condolences.

"Thank you." Ilse looked down at the knitting project she clutched in her lap. "As for the rest of it, I know it was irresponsible to run away, but this town was so judgmental and oppressive—everybody is always in your business. I wanted to see what the rest of the world was like. Outside of Larkston, I felt free. I could make my own choices. But as the years passed, I grew more and more ashamed. I knew that you must be hurting. There were many times when I thought of coming back, but I didn't want to see in your eyes what I'm seeing right now." Her expression grew softer.

Bibi nodded.

"And I couldn't call because I never felt as though I had the right words. Especially when mom died." Ilse fumbled with the yarn for a moment. "Turns out, I still don't have the right words. But I am incredibly sorry for everything. All of it. I never meant to hurt you." She looked up at Bibi. Tears shone in her eyes.

Bibi cleared her throat. "Thank you. I'm glad you came back."

Her simple response was admirable. No accusations, no lectures, no descriptions of the pain she had endured—just a straightforward, unconditional welcome.

Ilse wiped at her eyes.

I wanted to ask why Ilse was in Larkston now, especially given the focus of the missing manuscript, but it didn't feel like it was my place to do so. Hopefully Bibi would get that information from her sister on her own once she thought about the timing.

Or once I mentioned it to her privately.

"Have you seen Alice yet? She was excited to see you last night," I said, trying to lighten the mood.

Ilse smiled. "No. I'll go over to the cottage soon. Darien is still...with us?"

"Alive and well." Bibi said reassuringly. "Stronger than ever."

"You know, in some ways, it feels like not a day has gone by...this house feels exactly the same, Bibi. You've done a terrific job of preserving it and keeping the family home in the family."

"Not *so* terrific—I'm putting it on the market soon."

"What? Why?"

"It's too expensive and too big for me to manage."

Ilse shook her head fiercely. "There's got to be a way. I think we have to save the homestead."

"It's almost a done deal," Bibi said. "I already have two buyers fighting over it."

"But you'll need my approval to go forward," Ilse said calmly.

"What are you talking about?" Bibi stared at her.

"Because I'm a Callahan too."

The room felt suddenly colder.

Chapter 13

Bibi came to the cottage as I was preparing for an appointment at Gillian's literary agency.

"I just checked the will, which left everything to Jamie."

"They named Jamie and not Jensen?"

"They were heartbroken when he left. Mr. Callahan was furious, and he immediately cut Jensen out of the will. Mrs. Callahan, however, privately asked Jamie to take care of his brother if he ever came back. Jamie would have done that anyway, and he did search for Jensen, for years and years. Even hired a private investigator. But I don't think Jensen wanted to be found." She sighed. "In any case, I'm happy to share everything. Half and half. Even if she hadn't married Jensen, she's my sister."

"Bibi, you should definitely talk about this with your lawyer before you discuss the issue any further with Ilse."

"I'll call him—and I'm not putting the house on the market until after the holidays, anyway."

"Good idea."

"I'm still floating about the fact that Ilse is back, after all. When she showed me the dove tattoo, I couldn't believe it. She got that down in Colorado Springs the day before she disappeared. It has to be her—I don't know who outside of our family would have even *seen* it. Ilse had taken a picture and pinned it to her bedroom wall, but my mother hid that before the police arrived. I don't think she told them about the tattoo as an identifying mark, she was so upset that Ilse had done it." She raised an eyebrow. "Back then, at least around here, tattoos were considered far more outrageous than they are now. Which is of course why Ilse did it."

"I'm glad you've been reunited."

She gave me a little hug. "Now if we can just sort out the inheritance, all will be well."

Spoken like every heiress in a historical novel who is about to get taken for everything she's worth.

I chided myself.

A familiarity with literary tropes can make one a bit paranoid.

The drive into Denver was rough. The roads were slick, snow was still falling, and if the weather got any worse, they might close I-25 before I made it back to Larkston. I realized, with a pang of disappointment, that I would need to head south immediately after the meeting, rather than stopping by one of my favorite bookstores downtown, as I'd planned.

I pulled up in front of the three-story rectangular building with brown wood siding in Cherry Creek shortly after noon. The trees out front were strung with white fairy lights and a green wreath with a red bow hung on the black door. The decorations weren't enough to fully restore joy after my foiled bookstore plans, but I admired the picturesque scene.

Inside, there was a young man with a crew cut in a snowman sweater behind a desk. "Hello! I'm Lars. May I help you?"

"Lila Maclean. I have an appointment with Hallie Tanaka."

Lars checked an appointment book and made a notation, then jumped up and led me past numerous offices to a larger one at the back. He murmured something to the occupant and gestured for me to go in, adding that if I needed anything to please let him know.

A woman with dark hair shot with gray looked up from her work. "Come in—I'm Hallie. And please excuse the sweater." Hers boasted an illuminated string of colorful lights. "I don't normally dress this way, but we're having our holiday party this afternoon. It seemed important to go ahead, despite everything. Gillian would definitely have wanted that."

I took the chair facing her desk. "Thank you for seeing me. As I mentioned on the phone, I'm trying to gather information about her."

"Are you a private investigator? I forgot to ask." She removed her glasses and set them on the desk next to a bowl of fragrant pinecones.

"No, just a friend. I've been asked to help out, see if we can find out what happened to her."

Hallie bowed her head and closed her eyes for a moment. "We're all shocked and saddened. Such a horrible thing. It still doesn't seem possible."

"I'm very sorry for your loss. Would you be willing to tell me about her?"

"Gillian was a wonderful woman. Remarkably talented—so many fabulous authors owe her their careers—and very kind. She donated a good portion of the agency's money to various charities."

"Can you think of anyone who might have had a grudge against her?"

"Honestly, no. Not even her employees. I've worked in publishing forever and can tell you that an agency with this type of culture is rare. I've never been at a company where the boss didn't get a little heat from disgruntled employees, but Gillian was the kind of person who always treated others with respect, and she expected us to do the same. She vetted her hires carefully and didn't bring in destructive people. We are a team and a family. It has made all the difference."

"What will happen to the agency now that she's...gone?"

"Nothing will change. She had already retired and handed over the reins to me."

"Who is managing her affairs?"

"Her lawyers, as far as I know. There is a cousin, I think, who may be on his way here. Someone else is arranging an event. I know I saw an email, but I can't remember..." she trailed off. "There's a lot going on."

"Oh, do you mean Bibi Callahan?" She'd told me as I was running out the door this morning that she was organizing a memorial service in Larkston on Friday.

"Yes, that's right. Also, we have decided to establish a community grant program in her name, so we'll let you know when that's up and running."

"Thank you. And call anytime if you happen to think of anything else." I gave her a business card.

She looked down at it. "Oh, I didn't know you were a professor at Stonedale. How wonderful. What do you teach?"

"American literature."

"Who's your favorite author? I always love asking professors that."

"Isabella Dare."

She looked surprised. "I don't think I've read her...or even heard of her."

"Most people haven't." I launched energetically into my introduction-to-Isabella speech.

"How fascinating." She handed me a card as well. "When you give your next talk on her, I'd love to attend. Keep me posted."

After a white-knuckle drive through the snow back down to

Larkston, I arrived in time for dinner. Ilse was out, so it was just the two of us. I took the opportunity to fill Bibi in on what I'd learned in Denver. It wasn't much aside from the fact that since Gillian had retired, there didn't seem to be a motive coming from the agency personnel. At least not one that I could see.

I told Bibi, too, about the grant program. "So glad to know that," she said. "I'll give Hallie a call and offer any help that I can with that."

She passed me a bowl of macaroni and cheese. I couldn't have ordered a better comfort food if I'd called ahead.

I took some steamed broccoli too to balance things out.

Watching the snow falling onto the drifts in the backyard was far more peaceful than driving in it. I admired the silent scene.

"The wind seems to be dying down," I said.

"Good. I hope it warms up again before the party. Not so much that the snow disappears, of course. One does need a *little* bit of snow around for a holiday party." Bibi smiled sadly. "Gillian used to say that snow was nature's way of decorating for the season."

"That's a lovely thought."

We ate in silence for a few moments.

"Have you heard any updates from the police, Bibi?"

"They have some leads, which they can't share, and they'll be in touch as soon as there is something they can."

"That sounds about right. They have a lot to process."

"Do you think—" Bibi abruptly stopped.

"What?"

"Do you think you would feel comfortable calling Lex, asking if he's heard anything?"

I could feel my jaw tighten despite myself.

Bibi waved her hands quickly, as if erasing the idea. "Never mind. Pretend I didn't say anything. I know you're broken up."

"You're fine. I just...can't. Plus, he wouldn't be able to tell us anything in addition to what the police are willing to say. He's not even in town."

"I know." She looked sheepish. "Maybe I wanted there to be a reason for the two of you to talk. You seemed so happy together at the conference last spring."

I rose, stiffly, and cleared my place. "Thank you for dinner. Do you want any help with the dishes?"

"I can manage. Would you like some coffee?"

"No, thank you. I have a headache—think I'll call it a night."

My head had indeed begun to throb as though a parade had claimed a route through my brain—no doubt due to the stress of the hours of driving in such horrid weather.

Or at least that's what I was willing to attribute it to.

That night, I dreamed I was standing on the bridge above Silver Rush Lake. It was dark, starry, and warm. I could hear footsteps, shouts, and the occasional burst of laughter. I turned to walk farther along the bridge, but my legs wouldn't work. No matter how much I tried, I couldn't move from the center spot. As the footsteps around me came closer, the sky went from deep blue to bright orange in a heartbeat. It became harder to breathe. Suddenly, the laughter turned to screams and my skin began to glow.

I sat up, covered in sweat. Heart pounding, I slipped out of bed and went to crack the window. The air that rushed in wasn't fresh and rejuvenating—it was acrid and thick. Smoke.

I slammed the window shut, coughing, and ran to the bedroom door, feeling the wood first to make sure it wasn't hot before cracking it cautiously open, just a sliver. A gray haze hung in the air near the ceiling, and the burning smell was even stronger out here. I couldn't see any fire yet, but I heard loud crackling above me. Terrified that the roof was about to collapse, I fell to the floor and crawled as quickly as I could to the front door, pausing only to pull my satchel off of the chair and shove my nearby phone into the back pocket. I grabbed my coat while slipping my feet into the boots by the table and turned the lock.

As soon as I wrenched the door open and stumbled away, I turned to see an orange blaze hungrily consuming the home. Black smoke billowed up from the structure as flames licked the surrounding trees.

While I sped up the path to the house, though I was sliding on the snow, I managed to hit the keys for 911. The operator told me to stay on the line after I'd reported the fire, so I dug around in my satchel with the other hand until I found the key Bibi had given me for Callahan House. I unlocked the door and ran upstairs, calling her name.

Bibi's bedroom door opened and she came out into the hallway, looking confused. As soon as she understood what was happening, she went to wake Ilse. I raced back downstairs and headed for Alice and Darien's house. When I thumped on their door, the porch lights came on.

"We know, child," Darien said, swinging the door halfway open while Alice peeked out from behind him. They were both fully dressed. "Thank you for checking on us."

"Come to the house," I urged.

"If the fire moves this way, we will." His mouth was set in a grim line.

"I think you should evacuate to be on the safe side."

He conferred with his wife. The sirens in the distance were growing louder.

"Go on back," Darien said. "Alice feels better here."

"Are you sure?"

"Yes. We will keep watch."

I could see his logic. It was about the same distance between the cottages and the main house, so either place was equally safe, theoretically, as long as the wind didn't shift and the fire didn't jump.

"Darien, please would you put my number in your phone? Then if you call me, I'll run back."

Not that I was a superhero or anything, but at least I could offer help if they needed me.

He pulled out his cell and typed in the numbers as I recited them.

"Done."

"Thank you."

The wail of the approaching fire engines grew louder. I scurried up the path to check on Bibi and Ilse, shaking.

By six a.m., the cottage was completely gone, along with a patch of trees surrounding it. Nearby pines were covered in soot, and the air had an oppressive chemical odor and taste. Items that had melted in the blaze were scattered on the ground, misshapen and forlorn.

"It was a good thing there was already snow on the trees and ground, or this could have taken down all three buildings," Bibi said. "At least that's what the captain told me."

"Thank goodness. Should we go back to the house? Do you want to try to get some sleep?"

"I don't think I could sleep right now. I need to talk to the insurance people, who are coming over later. I've already set up one of the guest rooms for you on the second floor for the remainder of your stay. I'm so sorry that you lost everything." She gripped my arm. "Oh no—your research!"

"My laptop and notebooks were in my satchel," I assured her. "Some books I was using were destroyed, but they can be replaced."

"But what about everything you own—"

"Bibi, please don't worry. The most important items were in my satchel, which I managed to bring with me out of there. I'll go back to Stonedale and get more clothes and things."

"You are being very kind, Lila." She squeezed my arm gently and turned back to the destruction. After a moment, she spoke softly, "You know, maybe there *is* a Callahan Curse."

"More likely that something happened with the furnace. We knew it wasn't working very well, right?"

"That's the most likely explanation, though I thought I'd fixed it." She chewed her lip. "You don't think someone would have set this fire on purpose, do you?"

"Why would they do that?"

"To send a message."

"What message?"

She faced me. "That someone is taking down the Callahans...and that I am next in line."

Bibi might be right, but it wouldn't do any good to add credence to that theory. "Or maybe it was a message for me since I was the one staying there. Remember, Tacey warned us both."

Bibi shook her head. "I can't imagine why anyone would ever want to hurt *you*."

That was the same thing everyone had been saying about Gillian, and look what happened to her.

Chapter 14

"How did it go?" Bibi asked several hours later, when I returned from Stonedale. The dark circles under her eyes were the same color as her dress, a sort of bruised maroon, and the white cardigan resting on her shoulders emphasized how pale she was.

"Fine, thanks." I set my battered old suitcase—glad I hadn't thrown it away when I bought a new one for sabbatical—down in the foyer next to the stairs. "I'm ready to help you with whatever you need today."

"It's terrible that you lost anything at all," Bibi said sadly. "Make a list and I'll include the items to be replaced in the insurance claim. The inspector has already been here, and I'm in the middle of the paperwork right now."

"Please don't worry about it."

"I *insist*."

I'd never hear those words again without thinking about Gillian. "Thank you, Bibi, and I'm so sorry, again, that you lost your cottage."

"We can always rebuild it. All that matters is that you are safe."

I didn't know how Bibi was able to remain so calm about everything, but she was truly an inspiration.

"Let's get you squared away." She led me up the stairs to a bedroom on the second floor. I was thrilled to see that she had chosen the round one directly above the library, which had a window seat running along the front, a bed so high there were steps required to climb into it, and a large wardrobe with pearl inlay. Everything shone in ruby and gold.

"That door," she pointed to the left, "opens into your closet, which you go through to get to the en suite. My room, in the east tower, is set up the same way, you may remember."

"It's gorgeous."

"I hope you enjoy. I'm not sure why I didn't ask if you'd rather stay in the house sooner. It didn't even occur to me."

"Oh, I was very happy in the cottage..." I trailed off, wincing. The last thing I wanted to do was remind her of the fire.

If that made her uncomfortable, she didn't show it. She smiled and turned to leave.

After I put my clothes away in the wardrobe, I returned downstairs and made her a cup of tea and carried it into the parlor. It was the least I could do.

"Thank you, kind soul." She put down the page she'd been reading and accepted the tray, which she set gently on the coffee table in front of her. Lifting up the cup, she took a long sip and closed her eyes. "Completely what the doctor ordered."

"Is there anything I can do?" Ilse appeared in the doorway. Her fuzzy sweater was a study in oranges ranging from light to dark. It was an odd choice for the day after a fire, I thought. Or maybe it wasn't. Everything felt exaggerated and overly meaningful today—my nerves were shot.

"Come in and talk to us, dear," Bibi said. "How are you doing?"

"I'm fine," Ilse replied, as she moved to sit next to Bibi on the sofa. "Considering."

"Not the best welcome I could have offered you," Bibi said ruefully. She took another sip.

"Forget about me. I'm more worried about you." Ilse studied her face.

"Don't be. I'm tough." Bibi smiled and put down her tea. She patted Ilse on the arm. "No one was hurt and that's the most important thing."

"Yes, though my heart is still broken. We grew up there!" Ilse's eyes filled up with tears.

Bibi's eyes filled up too.

I went back to the kitchen, leaving them to their memories, and poured Ilse a cup of tea. I didn't even know if she liked tea, but that was what one offered in times like this.

The doorbell rang when I was returning to the parlor. I told Bibi I'd answer it, handed Ilse the tea, and opened the door.

Detective Ortiz was there with another officer. His black suit and her regulation blue jacket were dusted with snow. I greeted them and stepped back as they came into the foyer.

"Bibi's in the parlor," I said, gesturing toward it.

They thanked me and entered the room.

"We have some news," Detective Ortiz said. He was carrying a bulging brown envelope.

The brunette beside him—Officer Scott, according to her nametag—asked if Bibi wanted to speak privately.

She indicated that she'd prefer we stay right where we were and invited them to sit down. They politely declined.

Detective Ortiz addressed Bibi. "A manuscript has been found—"

She made a sound in her throat.

"—that we think may be the one you reported missing from your home. We wondered if you could confirm that for us." He handed Bibi the package.

"Where did you find it?" She glanced at him while opening the top.

"It was mailed to the station."

"Someone turned it *in* after stealing it last week?" She stopped in the middle of removing the pages from the envelope.

He shrugged.

Once she had removed the manuscript, she flipped through it and smiled. "Yes, this is it."

"Are you sure?" Officer Scott asked.

"Yes."

"And you *are* the author of the manuscript? You're Isabella Dare?" Officer Scott asked, an edge in her voice.

"Why does that matter?"

"It matters."

Bibi looked back and forth between them. "Yes, I am Isabella Dare. But it's not widely known, and I prefer to keep it that way."

"We'll do what we can." Detective Ortiz stepped forward. "But we are going to need you to come with us, Professor Callahan."

"Why?"

"You're not under arrest, but based on what that manuscript says, we have some questions for you. I'll need the manuscript back too, if you don't mind." He held out his hand and she returned the envelope.

"Surely there's been some mistake," Ilse protested. "Also, your timing is terrible. My sister has been through quite enough in the past twenty-four hours. You do know that we had a fire here last night, right?"

"Couldn't you speak with her here?" I seconded Ilse.

"I'm sorry about that, but we were asked to bring her in," Officer Scott said. She rested her hand on the gun in her side holster. It may have been an unconscious gesture, but I knew there was no way we were going to be able to stop them from taking Bibi to the station.

"Well then," Bibi said, resigned. "Let's get this over with."

* * *

"Wait until I get my hands on Mercy Throckham. I've left her ten messages already, and that little coward won't return my calls." Ilse was pacing back and forth in the library fuming about the fact that Tacey's daughter had taken over *Larkston Live* and posted a new article: "Stolen Manuscript Tells All!"

I didn't mind her change of venue, as I preferred the club chairs and shelves of books to the formal parlor furniture, but she was making me dizzy the way she was moving around the room. I twisted to face her. "Do you think the police leaked it to Mercy?"

"Of course. Nothing is sacred in this town. That's why I left in the first place."

"Is there anything we can do to help her?"

"Everyone knows the manuscript exists," Ilse swatted at the air, "and there's no stuffing *that* cat back into the bag."

"True."

"But perhaps even worse, she accuses the Hurston character based on Hudson Shane, of killing Elsa, the character based on me."

Mercy hadn't revealed anything about the book other than that detail, which was obviously tantalizing from a gossip perspective. I didn't believe that Mercy had read the whole thing—or she would certainly have discussed other plot points. It was more likely that her source fed her the most damaging part, or only what they could manage to share.

Unfortunately, it was an element that had police looking at Bibi differently than they had before.

"I am alive and well, as everyone can see for themselves. Therefore, Hudson isn't a murderer, and it's slanderous to repeat such nonsense." Ilse sank down in the chair opposite mine. "She should know better."

"Unless that's *not* why she repeated it," I said slowly. "Maybe the reason they took Bibi in for questioning has more to do with Hudson."

Ilse squinted at me. "I'm lost. Spell it out for me."

"Because of how Hudson died. The general agreement around here is that someone ran him off the road. If the police thought, after having read the manuscript, that Bibi *believed* Hudson killed you, then perhaps they are interpreting *his* death as revenge taken for *your* death."

"But Jamie died too that night. He was her entire world."

"Maybe they think that if she was cold-blooded enough to kill someone in the first place, she was cold-blooded enough to dispatch of her husband in the process, thereby inheriting Callahan House and everything that came with it, which could be viewed as a powerful motive as well."

"Oh." She covered her mouth with her hand. "That's terrible."

"Of course, we know she would never do any of that," I hastened to add.

"No, she most definitely would not." Ilse pushed herself out of the chair. "I'm going to the police station. Want to join me?"

"Yes. Unless you think someone should stay here."

"Let's go together. And let's swing by Mercy Throckham's place on the way. She's probably still there and I want to tell her a thing or two."

Fifteen minutes later, I was reluctantly following Ilse into the *Larkston Live* office. I sensed that it was a mistake, but I couldn't seem to stop the force of nature that was Ilse Callahan.

It was a small operation, with three chairs lined up near the door, presumably forming a waiting room, facing a reception desk. Behind that were three oversized wooden desks in a U-shape in the middle of the room. File cabinets took up the left wall, and the right side boasted a table with a coffee pot, a refrigerator, and a printer.

A slender young woman with bright orange hair pulled into a short ponytail was typing on a laptop at the desk facing us. Black eyeshadow matched both her lipstick and her short, ragged nails. Her shabby sweater was dark as well, with rows of safety pins attached at random intervals creating a vintage punk effect. She paused and said hello.

"Mercy Throckham?" Ilse stomped forward. I caught the fabric on the back of her coat, trying to slow her down, but it slipped through my fingers.

She watched us approach. "Yes. Who are you?"

"I am Ilse Smithson Callahan."

Mercy looked intrigued. "Ilse *Smithson*? The one who disappeared?"

"Yes."

She narrowed her eyes. "But you're alive now?"

Ilse sputtered. "What do you mean? You think I'm a ghost?"

Mercy sat back and crossed her arms. "Last I heard, you were dead."

"I'm standing right here, aren't I?" Ilse held her arms out to her sides. "Looks like that was some bad reporting."

Mercy scowled. "Before my time. And did you say Callahan too?"

"Yes, I married Jensen Callahan."

Mercy's overly plucked eyebrows rose.

I had never seen anyone raise their hackles as fast as these two had at each other. The sooner we got out of here, the better. I nudged Ilse, hoping she'd take the hint to bring the energy down a little bit.

Ilse perched on one of the empty desks. "I'm here because of what you wrote about Bibi...and Hudson. How dare you?"

Mercy closed her laptop slowly and met Ilse's gaze. "I report it as I hear it."

"How can you sit there so calmly while there are serious consequences happening as we speak? My sister is at the police station!"

I nudged Ilse again. We didn't want to give Mercy any more information that she could use in her blasts.

Mercy stood up and came around her desk. The sweater was cropped at the waist, where her indigo miniskirt began. Her black tights had a run down to the top of her ankle-high boot. "This is my job. Rest assured that I am trying to be more objective than my predecessor—"

"I'm sorry about your mother, Mercy," I said quietly.

Ilse muttered something along the same lines.

Mercy gave me a grateful look. "But we still need to share the news in this town. We need to know who our neighbors are and what's taking place within our community. Unlike my mother, I *did* actually attend journalism school."

"Then why does your reporting come off as sensationalistic as hers was?" Ilse pursed her lips. "I've only been back for a few days and even I know she was off the rails. My sister has filled me in on all of the histrionic headlines and absurd innuendos that have been posted, particularly about the Callahans and the so-called curse."

"I can't speak to my mother's style, God rest her soul, but I will assure you I merely follow the story. Much depends on the facts I'm working with. Some are naturally more sensational than others."

"No." Ilse pointed a finger at her. "Admit it. You pick out the juiciest things and twist them all around just to sell papers."

"We're digital, not print." Mercy retorted, pushing back her uneven bangs.

"You know what I mean...attract advertisers. Get hits. Principle's the same."

Mercy shrugged. “It is a business, after all.”

Ilse sniffed. “I think you might extend more compassion to people who are in pain.”

“Mmm hmm.” Mercy examined one of her fingernails. “Likewise. If you’d ever like to do an interview about where you’ve been all of these years and why you never let a *single* person know where you were—even though they were grieving your death—give me a call.”

Ilse made a sound of exasperation. “That’s none of your business.” She climbed down and moved swiftly toward the front of the office, pausing to shout over her shoulder, “Stop messing with my family!”

Bibi emerged through the front doors of the police station. She climbed into the passenger seat and let out a deep breath, as if she’d been holding it the whole time she’d been inside.

She put on her seatbelt silently.

“What happened?” Ilse pulled out of the parking lot.

“They asked me over and over again why I’d written what I did. You’d think at least one of them would understand the basic idea of fictionalization, but they kept treating everything I’d written as fact.”

“It *was* based on fact, though,” Ilse reminded her.

“Yes, but also a high degree of imagination and speculation. And we know that I was completely wrong, don’t we, Ilse?”

“What do you mean?”

“Hudson didn’t kill you! You’re here! I kept repeating that—it’s extremely obvious, isn’t it?—but they acted as though it was beside the point.”

“Because it might be beside the point to them, if our theory is right,” I said to Bibi.

"What theory?" She twisted in her seat to look at me.

I hesitated.

"Just say it," Bibi urged me.

"Perhaps after reading the manuscript, they believe that you thought Hudson killed Ilse, so you killed Hudson by forcing him off of the road. As revenge."

Bibi gasped. "Oh no. They never came out and said why they were harping on that so much, but that makes perfect sense." She stared at the road ahead, processing. The windshield wipers moved back and forth, their monotonous sound strangely hypnotic. "You both know I didn't do that, right? Why would I? My husband was in that car!"

We assured her that we knew she was innocent.

"I need to call my lawyer immediately when we get home. He'll know what to do."

"You didn't call him already?" Ilse asked incredulously.

"I wasn't arrested. It didn't seem necessary."

"You might want to ask your lawyer to get a copy of the manuscript," I suggested. "If they're going to use it to go after you, it seems important to review exactly what you wrote. You said before that you haven't looked at it in years."

"Good idea," Bibi said wearily. "Oh, this is overwhelming."

"In light of everything, do you want to cancel the party?" I asked Bibi. "You have so much on your plate already."

"No. I'm looking forward to it. It's my favorite event of the year. Plus, this is my final year of hosting. I couldn't possibly cancel." She turned around and faced me. "I only hope people will still come. Mercy may have scared them all away with her curse talk."

Just then, our phones went off at the same time. Mercy had posted a new article: "Ilse Callahan Returns; Home Burns to the Ground!"

"She makes it sound like I burned down our house," Ilse fumed, shaking her phone. "What is *wrong* with her?"

"We know you didn't do it," Bibi consoled her.

I started to say something but was struck by a thought: *did* we know for sure that Ilse wasn't involved? The fire occurred soon after she arrived at Callahan House.

It wasn't the time or place to pursue that line of conversation, though. Ilse was trashing Mercy in a white-hot rage and Bibi was trying to calm her, saying it was the furnace that was responsible for the cottage burning and the firefighter's report would prove it.

I looked at the lake as we went over the bridge, then at the empty spot where the guest cottage used to be, surrounded by bare branches and darkness. In the waning light of the day, it was as melancholy a place as could be imagined.

Chapter 15

By the next morning, Bibi was invigorated. Her demeanor might have been considered puzzling by some—in the past week alone, one of her best friends had been murdered, her long-lost sister had returned, her family home had burned to the ground, and she'd been questioned by police. Yet here she was in the dining room, folding napkins and chattering away about party plans.

That wasn't the sign of something dark, was it? I instantly pushed that question away, irritated at myself for even thinking it. Bibi had never shown a single indication of a personality disorder or anything of the sort. She was just exceptionally adept at managing difficulties that came her way.

"We have much to do. Committee members will be in and out of Callahan House from now until Saturday night," Bibi said, "but we always kick things off with our traditional Lark brunch on the Wednesday before the party. We unpack the indoor decorations—they're the only ones I trust with the antiques."

"Everything looks beautiful."

She had set the table with a cheery red tablecloth. White china plates banded with silver waited at each place, along with polished silverware, napkin rings made of twisted silver, and crystal goblets with silver stems. Silver pinecones in a silver filigree bowl rested between two silver lanterns that glowed softly.

"The Callahans liked to visibly honor their ancestors' good luck in the silver rush," she said, winking at me. "All silver, all the time on *their* holiday table. We're paying homage to that tradition one last time."

"That's where the name of Silver Rush Lake comes from as well, I assume?"

"Yes. Good old Godfrey. Not one for humility." Her eyes rested on a portrait in the hallway that I'd never looked closely at before. Godfrey stood perfectly upright, staring at the viewer. A silver watch chain was visible across the black vest he wore below a long red coat. His dark top hat was straight, and he had a silver pin tucked vertically into his tie. Gloves were clutched in one hand; the other held a whip. I didn't even want to know what that was for.

His expression was neutral, but it was easy to sense that here was a man who didn't take no for an answer.

Maybe it was the whip.

"Is Godfrey going riding?"

Bibi stopped folding to consider my question. "I have no idea. I always took the whip as more metaphorical than literal, though you might be right."

"Hellooooooo!" Margot's voice reached us from the foyer. "We're here!"

Bibi handed me the last two napkins and went to greet her guests. I folded and placed them inside the rings as she had done, though the result was less a sophisticated sculptural shape, like Bibi's, and more a crunched-up wad of fabric. Oh well. At least we weren't being graded on it.

I went to say hello to everyone, and soon, we were gathered around the table with plates full of frittata, salad, and fruit.

"Cinnamon bun, anyone?" Penelope asked, passing a stoneware platter. "I whipped them up this morning. I thought, given the week you've had, Bibi, you might appreciate a little sweetness."

Bibi thanked her profusely and we all took one of the warm spirals oozing with sweet glaze. The smell brought back memories of Christmas morning with my mother and Calista—cinnamon buns were an annual tradition.

I tasted it and had to repress a groan. They were magnificent.

The other women asked Bibi about the fire.

"It's terribly sad, I know, but what's done is done, and it could have been much worse."

"That's true," came a voice from the hallway. The women looked over, politely waiting for her to be identified, I suppose. No one seemed to recognize her at first.

Then Margot gasped. "Ilse? Is that you?"

Penelope stared.

She held out her arms. "Yes, it's me. Hello. Good to see you both."

The Larks hurried over to hug and gush over her. They were still exuberantly professing surprise and peppering her with questions when Bibi said, "Should we give her a chance to sit down?"

They returned to their places and Ilse took a chair at the end of the table across from Bibi, who jumped up again to make her a plate. Margot and Penelope continued their questions until it had been established that Ilse had run away with Jensen and was now back from California.

"This is bewildering," Margot said. "I mean, I saw the article online that you were back, but it's a completely different thing to see you in the flesh. It's positively uncanny."

"I'm glad you're okay," Penelope said, shyly.

"Are you staying at Callahan House?" Margot asked, "For good?"

Ilse and Bibi locked eyes, and something passed between them.

"I hope you will," Bibi said. "We haven't discussed it yet, but it's as much your home as mine."

Ilse gave her a broad smile. "Thank you."

We ate in silence for a spell, then Margot spoke. "Speaking of articles, did you all see that Mercy Throckham has taken over the *Larkston Live* site? I thought the drama would go when Tacey did." She winced, then added hastily, "God rest her soul, of course."

"She claimed that she'll be less sensationalistic than her mother," Ilse said. "Time will tell."

"When did she say that?" Bibi asked, confused.

"When Lila and I talked to her yesterday."

Bibi looked at me.

"We stopped by on the way to the police station," I explained.

"You'll be glad to hear that I told Mercy off," Ilse said. "She had no right to post that story about your book."

"Thank you." Bibi smiled at her.

"Back up, please. Why did you go to the police station?" Margot tore off the tiniest morsel of cinnamon bun and ate it daintily.

I apologized for having blurted out that information, but Bibi said it was fine and recounted the events in detail. Once she'd reached the end, she led the others into the great room to begin unpacking the decorations.

I stayed behind and cleaned everything up, as penance.

When the last dish had been put away, I joined the Larks—and Ilse—in the great room. They were gathered next to an enormous pine tree in the corner; its pungent scent filled the room. There was a barely perceptible undertone of smoke that I hoped would fade over the next few days. If not, a cozy fire in the hearth during the party could masquerade as the source.

"The tree is gorgeous!" I said to Bibi.

"Darien set it up this morning," Bibi replied happily. "We have ornaments representing a variety of holidays celebrated around the world during the season. There's a box of hooks on the coffee table. Let's unwrap them and start hanging." For the better part of an hour, we did what she said, until almost every inch of the tree was covered.

Then we tackled the boxes she'd dragged out of storage. Amidst the careful layers of tissue paper were more treasures: decorative ropes of multicolored crystals to hang along the walls in graceful waves; carved wooden reindeers to stand in a row near the window; brass, silver, and gold candleholders for tabletops; wreaths galore; and a stunning selection of stained glass bells to hang from the foyer chandelier.

Eventually, everything had been unpacked and distributed throughout the first floor of Callahan House. Bibi asked us if we'd like to sit and enjoy the fruits of our labors in the great room while she made some coffee and tea. Ilse offered to help her and the rest of us sat on the large sectional sofa near the fireplace.

Penelope picked up a book from the stack on the coffee table and leafed idly through it.

"Oh, wow, here we all are," she exclaimed, turning the book so we could see a full-page picture of the Larks and their beaus dressed up for a formal dance. We crowded around as she identified everyone.

"What book is that?" Margot asked her.

"A history of the college written by Bibi's mother-in-law," Penelope replied, flipping through the pages more rapidly. "Oh, here's another one." The group was seated on the steps of the library.

"And what does Dana Callahan say about us?" Margot asked, taking the book from her.

"The caption says, 'Callahan students are our future.'" Penelope smiled.

"She was proud of Jamie, that's for sure." Margot closed the cover and slid the book back onto the table. "I think she hoped he would be town mayor one day."

"Or running the college," Penelope added.

"Is that what Jamie wanted to do?" I asked.

"He was happy teaching literature. I don't think he shared any of the dreams his mother had for him," she replied.

"Honestly, all Jamie cared about was being married to Bibi." Margot laughed. "That was his primary goal. He always said it was love at first sight."

Penelope agreed.

"Speaking of a walk down memory lane, I still can't believe Ilse's here. It's been ages," Margot said, readjusting her deep red silk scarf, which drew my attention to it.

"I know. It feels like she's returned from the dead, because that's how we thought of her for so long." Penelope wore a woven scarf, too, with an embroidered holly pattern.

Frankly, I was surprised to see everyone still wearing scarves. After Gillian and Tacey's deaths, I had decided to put my own away for the season, which I thought was prudent.

"She seems the same," Penelope continued. "Feisty as ever."

"Why come back now, I wonder? After all these years?" Margot arched her eyebrow.

"Well, she's a widow. Maybe she was lonely and missed home." Penelope played with the fringe on her scarf. "It happens."

"Or maybe she heard that Bibi had inherited everything and wanted a piece of it," Margot said.

"She did bring that up right away," I said. "That she was a Callahan too."

"See?" Margot crowed. "People don't change. She *always*

wanted whatever Bibi had."

"I wonder if Bibi ever found out about Ilse and Jamie," Penelope mused.

There was a crash behind us. When we turned around, Bibi was staring, open-mouthed, over the shards of a teapot.

The next few minutes were chaos. I ran over to comfort Bibi, but Ilse was already there, denying that anything had ever happened with Jamie; Margot was yelling at Penelope for raising the ugly rumor in the first place; and Penelope was defending herself for repeating gossip and apologizing to Bibi, who was saying that she had heard the persistent rumor but knew without a doubt that it wasn't true.

I turned to the mess on the floor.

After things quieted down, Bibi thanked us for our efforts and asked Ilse if she would help her return the empty boxes to the storage area downstairs. The Larks and I offered assistance, but she said she'd taken enough of our time already and that we should feel free to go. It was said with affection but felt like a command. I wondered if it had been a strain, keeping up a brave face in front of her friends, especially when it became impossible to do so at the end.

Perhaps it wasn't that she was uncommonly capable of handling problems. Perhaps she was just gifted at *seeming* as though they didn't bother her. Which would be more denial than management.

As I walked upstairs to give them some time alone, my phone buzzed. I looked at the screen and was shocked to see a text from Lex: *We need to talk.*

My heart did a funny dip, as though it were plummeting downward into the thick carpet below my feet. I grabbed ahold of the bannister and took several deep breaths to steady myself. Did I want to talk to him?

I honestly wasn't sure.

Part of me was thrilled to hear from him. Another part was annoyed that he was contacting me. But most of all, I was curious.

I typed *Talk about what?* and stared at the screen for a while, trying to decide whether or not to send it.

With a start, I remembered that if he was watching, those pesky three dots would be visible.

I knew from experience that it was confusing to be on the receiving end if those dots hovered for a long time as if the sender was composing a lengthy text, but no message followed.

Quickly, I deleted my response and closed his message.

He could try and interpret what that meant all night long as far as I was concerned.

At dinner, Ilse fussed over a subdued Bibi. It made sense that she was quiet—she was under a tremendous amount of stress and undoubtedly exhausted. Yet whenever I came close to mentioning what had happened earlier, Bibi blocked it with the precision of a practiced fencer, steering all inquiries instead toward the subject of the upcoming party.

She'd gone from an open book to a closed one.

I finally asked Ilse to tell us more about her life before coming to Larkston, trying to change the subject, but she said she was tired and would have to take a raincheck.

The sisters seemed to be circling their wagons.

But why would I be on the outside all of a sudden?

I finished eating without raising any other topics of discussion and cleared my place.

When I tried to help Bibi wash the dishes, Ilse shooed me gently but firmly out of the kitchen.

Chapter 16

Thursday flew by, with party planners coming over to meet with Bibi. She was back to her old self, perky as ever, and asked me to sit in on a number of the meetings in order to help her keep them on schedule. Some of the committee members, she confided, tended to blather on and on if there wasn't an end time in sight. My job was to clear my throat and remind her that she had another meeting soon. Our system worked smoothly, for the most part.

Late in the afternoon, I answered the door, expecting a party planner to be standing there. Margot strode past me instead, calling Bibi's name. Her anger rolled off of her in invisible but potent waves.

"How are you?" I reached out to take the coat she was shrugging off.

"She knows I'm here. I texted her on the way. We need to talk." She slapped her gloves and craned her neck down the hallway, calling Bibi's name again.

"I'm here, Margot." Bibi's voice reached us from the library. "Come in. I'm looking for one of my decorations. Did you see it when we unpacked? A small porcelain figurine of carolers? I wanted to show my sister."

Margot rolled her eyes and stomped into the room. "No, I didn't see your statue. And we have more important things to talk about. Guess where I spent the entire afternoon? At the police station. Being questioned. Like a *criminal*." She spit out the last word.

Bibi's mouth formed a small "o."

"All because of your book."

"Did you see the manuscript?" I asked.

"No. They wouldn't let me touch it. But they grilled me about that fight with Gillian back in high school. What were you trying to do, ruin my reputation?" She glared at Bibi and pointed. "It's a good thing you aren't wearing a scarf right now, or I'd strangle you myself!"

Bibi and I gasped.

Margot froze. "Sorry. That was too far."

Neither one of us spoke.

She looked back and forth between our shocked faces. "Come on. You know I would never do that. I'm not a *murderer*."

Bibi walked over to the club chairs. She gestured for us to join her. "I'm sorry for writing about that. I never meant for the book to be seen. I was writing through my feelings."

Margot sighed. "I know. However, it *has* been seen, and as a result, the police are looking at me for Gillian's murder."

"Again, I apologize. I know you didn't do it."

I wondered how Bibi knew that—anyone could have done it—but kept that thought to myself.

Bibi went on. "We all know you don't have a violent bone in your body."

Margot nodded. "I'm sorry I lashed out at you, Bibi. It was a humiliating experience. To be treated like a guilty party is horrible."

"I understand."

"I know you do, having been hauled down to the station yourself. All the more reason that we," Margot gave her a steely look, "have to do everything in our power to keep that manuscript from coming out. If that's what happened to us based on one small part, it would be a disaster if the entire book were available."

Bibi agreed.

"The good news is that they've interviewed us both now, and they don't have enough evidence to accuse either one of us."

"I'm not sure it works like—" I began, but Margot sped on.

"Looking at us is futile."

"Though sometimes innocent people are unfairly convicted," Bibi said.

"Right. Listen, Bibi, you should make it known that you are Isabella Dare. It's going to come out anyway, eventually. Don't you want to be the one who controls how that happens? Don't you agree, Lila?" Margot cut her eyes toward Bibi and back, encouraging me to join in.

"It's something to consider." I wanted Bibi to do whatever she was comfortable with, so I wasn't going to push.

Margot rolled her eyes again, this time at me.

"Why do you think I should reveal myself now?" Bibi asked her.

"If they know you're keeping one secret, my dear, they know you are capable of keeping others."

She had a point there.

As Margot was leaving, a taxi pulled up. I watched, waiting to see which committee member would disembark. The steady stream of party preparation appointments was seemingly endless.

You could have knocked me over with a feather when my mother climbed out instead. The driver opened the trunk and set down an oversized red suitcase, which she towed behind her, bumping over the ice lumps. When she caught sight of me, she left it standing on the sidewalk and ran forward with open arms.

"Darling! It's me!"

I met her on the front porch, and we hugged. A cloud of perfume surrounded me—something boldly floral. She pulled back and studied my face, then patted my cheek and asked me to get her suitcase. I wrestled the heavy bag up the steps while she issued warnings about being careful. It wasn't clear if she meant me or the cargo, but eventually we were both inside the house.

"Surprise!" she sang, wiping the snowflakes out of her copper curls. "I'm here to celebrate the holidays with you."

"How wonderful!"

"I know how much you love surprises."

That was entirely untrue, but no matter how many times I told her that I did not love surprises, she maintained that of course I did, that *everybody* did, and that anyone who said they didn't was mistaken.

I hugged her again.

She peeled off her black coat and looked around for somewhere to put it. I stowed it away in the closet and closed the door. She wore a long dark dress with hand-painted gold crescent moons and an armful of gold bangles.

"Do you like my hair, darling?" She patted the ends, which fell just below her shoulders. She'd cut off at least fifteen inches since the last time I'd seen her.

"It's beautiful."

"I donated it last week and feel so much lighter—in *spirit* as well as *coiffure*. I don't know why it took me fifty-some years to work up the nerve to go shorter. Maybe at my next visit, I'll turn blonde. Or pink. Who knows what the future holds?" She spun around, peering down the hallway, and looking up the stairs. "My, this is grand, Lila. Calista said Callahan House was big, but she didn't do it justice."

"Calista told you about it?"

"Yes. I went to Stonedale University first to surprise you and your cousin, but the woman in the front office of the English department wouldn't tell me where you were. I tried to get it out of her, but she didn't budge."

I blanched, imagining my mother pumping Glynnis Klein for information. Though if anyone could handle her with grace and finesse, it would be Glynnis.

"Didn't you see the card on my door that said I was on sabbatical this semester?"

"Oh, I was *tired*, Lila, from flying *across the country.* I wasn't up to playing Nancy Drew, searching for clues everywhere. That's your gig."

I sighed.

"Anyway, then your *adorable* friend Nate showed up—I didn't know your offices were right next to each other, how divine! I'd forgotten how handsome he is." She winked. "He reminded me that you were on sabbatical, then he walked me down to Calista's office, and she took me out to lunch at Peak House. You know, they have the most *scrumptious* cheese plate. The fig jam alone was worth traveling thousands of miles for..." Given my family's affinity for cheese plates, I knew that there was no point interrupting her detailed review, which went on for some time as I led her into the parlor.

When Bibi came in from the kitchen, she smiled and held her arms out. "Violet! I haven't seen you in years. What a magnificent surprise."

My mother swooped over to hug Bibi—her expression en route said she counted this as new proof that everyone loves surprises. It also said she hoped I had noticed what Bibi said. And also that she knew I had.

The two of them exchanged updates on people and places unknown to me. Finally, Violet said, "Thanks for taking in my daughter this fall."

"It's been my pleasure. I'll miss her when she leaves."

"And when will that be?" Violet perched on the edge of the sofa and twisted her head up, like an inquisitive bird.

"Sunday," I said. "I would have left earlier, but Bibi asked me to stay through the holiday party."

"It's an annual tradition," Bibi said. "And the last year I'm hosting it, I'm afraid. I'm selling Callahan House."

"Oh, but it's *spectacular*," Violet replied, fluttering her hand around, presumably at the spectacularness. "Why would you ever sell it?"

"It's time."

I was struck by the flatness with which Bibi said it, as if she had disconnected emotionally. Perhaps that was the only way for her to move forward.

"Well, your decorations are *sublime*," Violet said. "This house should be photographed for a magazine."

"You still haven't said what prompted your trip out west. I'm thrilled that you're here for the holidays, but is everything okay?" Knowing my mother's propensity for impulsive actions, I almost dreaded hearing the answer.

"Can't a mother want to see her daughter and niece without needing a reason?"

"Of course."

"Also, the art-in became a nightmare…"

Aha!

"A squabble over facial appointments at one of our spa-inspiration events"—she explained her long-held theory about how spa days opened one's third eye and led to enhanced creative production—"introduced a flood of negative energy, which turned into a battle over paints and clay and studio time. It got so bad that my best friend Daphne—"

Frenemy, I corrected silently.

"—got into a screaming match and someone broke a palette over her head, and that was the beginning of the end."

Bibi looked alarmed.

"I don't think we'll come together for an art-in again, sadly." After a beat, Violet brightened up. "But seeing Daphne with paint streaming down her face was something I'll always cherish. Almost makes up for her little *digs* about the schedule that I worked so hard to put together. She thought I didn't hear them, but I did. Anyway, I missed you and now I'm free for the holidays, so here I am. I can't wait to have an old-fashioned Christmas celebration with you and your cousin, darling. Calista is very excited."

I smiled at her. "I'm excited too. In the meantime, I'll give you my keys, and you can stay at my place."

"Or," Bibi said, "you can stay here. We have plenty of room. Unless you're seeking some peace and quiet..."

If there was anything my mother didn't seek, ever, it was peace and quiet. She was a smack-dab-in-the-middle-of-things kind of person all the way.

"How generous," Violet said, clasping her hands. "I'd love to stay here, Bibi. Isn't this *terrific*, Lila?"

I didn't know how to bring up the fact that she, along with the rest of us, would be staying in a house where a murder had recently taken place. I didn't want to upset Bibi or dim the effect of her hospitality, but it did seem like the sort of thing that should at least be mentioned to a potential guest. In all likelihood, it wouldn't faze my mother at all; she probably would find the accommodations even more intriguing, given her penchant for noir. When we had a chance to speak privately, I would fill her in later. I hadn't told her about Gillian earlier because, well, what could she have done from New York besides worry about her daughter who had stumbled over yet another body? That sort of thing tended to weigh on a mother's mind, as she'd mentioned multiple times.

They went to set her up in one of the guest bedrooms. I was put in charge of lugging the hefty suitcase up the stairs—what was in there, anyway, lumps of coal for my stocking? With every bump, I reminded myself that I was an adult who could handle whatever life threw my way. I adored my mother, but she did tend to need more attention than most, and I wasn't sure I had much attentiveness in me, what with trying to solve a murder and help ensure that my hostess did not go to jail for it.

After more committee members came and went, Bibi's lawyer arrived and the two of them ducked into the library. Larry Birkenbee was a round, ebullient fellow with a rosy face and a gray beard whose vest with thick wide stripes peeking out from his somber suit put me in mind of a carnival barker. When he left, Bibi asked me to follow her to the study, where she handed me a folder.

"Would you still like to take a look at *The Secrets of Everwell*?"

"You have a copy? Don't you want to read it first?"

"I do now, thanks to Larry, but I have a thousand party details to follow up on, emails to answer, phone calls to make. You'll have to read it here—it has to be locked up again after you're done."

"In the same drawer?"

She shrugged. "It's secure. The manuscript was only stolen the first time because Gillian brought the key into the study."

"We think."

"It's pretty clear that Gillian—or the thief—used the key to unlock the drawer. In either scenario, it boils down to the key being in the room. Since I now have possession of the key, we should be fine."

I started to apologize again about mishandling the key before, but Bibi cut me off. "Just heard how that sounded. I didn't mean for it to suggest, in any way, shape, or form, as though I was blaming you. I don't blame you. Please take that to heart, dear." She looked at me intently until I nodded.

"It's just—"

"I know. If only this or that had been different. We all have regrets. But we cannot change anything, and we are not the ones who killed her. We *must* move on." She gave me a quick hug, then waved the folder around. "Would you like to read it now?"

I hesitated and avoided looking at the spot where Gillian was found. I'd already come into the study since they took her away, but I'd made it quick. In and out. Zip, zip. It wasn't the first time I'd had to spend time in a space where someone had passed away, but this room felt different somehow. Maybe there was something to Margot's assertions that the violence had left some sort of traces behind.

"Lila? I need to—"

"Sorry, yes." I reached out for the key and walked over to the desk.

"Let me know when you're done, and I'll lock it up." She bustled out of the room.

I sat down, opened the folder, and turned to chapter one.

An icy sensation rolled up my spine, and the lights flickered.

"Stop it. I have to read," I said.

To whom or to what, I didn't know.

Chapter 17

Three hours later, I leaned back from the desk and stretched my arms over my head. Bibi had used a pseudonym for everyone in the manuscript, but it was something close to their own name and easy to guess. Instead of Bibi, Jamie, Ilse, Margot, Winston, Penelope, Brody, Hudson, and Gillian, the characters were Barbi, Johnny, Elsa, Margie, Walton, Polly, Brydon, Hurston, and Ginny.

I had quickly settled into the rhythm of the novel—it had the same familiar style and pace as the other Isabella books I'd studied for so long. Athena Bolt is drawn into a murder mystery which begins with the body of Elsa discovered in the forest. One by one, Athena interviews the teenagers, a close-knit group of friends who held their last bonfire of the summer on the same night Elsa died. During her conversations, she hears accusations of betrayal, perceived injustices, and other secrets that thicken the suspect pool. At the end of the book, she gathers them into a circle at the site of their last bonfire and performs a dramatic reveal.

The conclusion that Hurston killed Elsa worked well for the novel, though in real life, Ilse's body had never been found, and Hudson hadn't been accused of murder. As far as I could tell, however, the particulars of the night lined up otherwise with what everyone had told me. It was undeniably eerie. Did they know more than they were saying?

I couldn't help feeling like I was missing something. My gaze wandered around the room as I turned over the plot points in my head and fell on a dark gray box in the far corner. I didn't remember seeing it when I'd organized the study, though I had diligently avoided the overstuffed chair in the corner because the muddy brown velvet emanated a repellent and sickly sweet odor. The box must have been tucked behind it; perhaps the police moved it when they processed the room.

I went over and picked up the metal box. It was about the size of a bread loaf and had a silver latch on the front side, which I flipped open. Inside were black-and-white photos of the people I'd just read about standing by trees, wading in the lake, holding firewood, and hoisting glass bottles. They looked so full of life and joy, smiling at the camera and each other—except for Hudson, with his perpetual sneer. The final picture was a group shot: Bibi, Margot, Penelope, and Gillian were in the front row with Winston, Hudson, and Brody in the back. Jamie must have taken that one.

After I pulled out my phone and captured the images, there was a knock at the door before it opened. Bibi asked how everything was going. She sounded uncertain, which surprised me. Perhaps she was anxious about what I'd learned. Or about what someone might think about her book in general.

"I'm done, and look what I found." I handed her the box.

"Oh! I haven't seen these in years." She flipped through them, putting a hand to her heart when she came to the group one.

"They're amazing."

"We were so young," she said softly.

"Was that the summer Ilse went missing?"

"It was the night you read about in the manuscript," she said. "At least the group one is. The rest were from earlier."

"Ilse wasn't there that night at all?"

"No, she was at the sleepover, which we all should have known was doomed from the start. It was out of character for her, sleeping at a girlfriend's house. She preferred to make her evening prowls alone."

Bibi put them back into the box and set it on one of the empty shelves. "I should frame those. Maybe I'll put pictures instead of art pieces on the shelf, as an homage to my friends."

I didn't have the heart to remind her that if she sold Callahan House, she wouldn't be filling those shelves at all.

"What did you think about the manuscript?"

"That's hard to answer, Bibi, because now I know it's based on real people."

"Let's put that part aside for now."

"From a scholarly perspective, then, I can't even put into words what it felt like to read the first-ever appearance of Athena Bolt. I loved it. I know you don't want to publish this, and I certainly understand why, but it has literary significance."

"Literary significance?" She waved that away. "The novels I *did* manage to get published don't even have that."

"My critical study of Isabella Dare argues at great length that they absolutely do. Also, they're beautifully written."

She laughed. "Well, once I get a chance to read your argument, maybe I'll be persuaded."

"And from a personal perspective, although I can see that it might be upsetting to air your teenage issues—who was jealous of whom and all that—and although the ending points a finger at an innocent party, it isn't anything you should feel guilty about. It's fiction."

"It was mostly a working out of the ideas swimming around in my head. I had a vague notion that I might rewrite it into a completely fictional novel down the road, but this first draft was only ever meant to be that. A recording of thoughts. A hypothetical."

"A hypothetical that was logical, actually. Based on the way that the character of Hurston acted in the book—bullying everyone all the time, not to mention cheating on his girlfriend—he did come across as the most likely villain."

"Well, Hudson wasn't a murderer. I wrote that because I was furious with him."

"Why?"

Bibi looked at her hands. "He was a bully—that part was true—but also he kept trying to convince Jamie to break up with me. I overheard him saying that I wasn't good enough for a Callahan. Not part of their world, is how he put it. Good enough for a high school fling but, he told Jamie, women of higher caliber awaited in college. Women who wouldn't embarrass the Callahan name."

"That's horrible."

She nodded. "When he drank, he got extra-snobby."

"That wasn't in the book, was it? The character of Hurston trying to convince Johnny to break up with Barbi, I mean."

"No. I couldn't bring myself to say it out loud. So I made Hurston the villain of the story instead. I guess you could say that I did take revenge on Hudson...in the fictional sense."

"It did make for a fascinating read." I went over to the desk and picked up the folder. "Your turn."

"I'll read it tomorrow. I'm too tired tonight to wade through any more words, especially those."

As she put the book in the drawer and locked it, I pulled up the pictures on my phone. When I swiped to the group shot, I noticed a blur in the background. Zooming into the tree branches behind the smiling faces revealed something: there was another face.

I gasped and showed Bibi. She opened the box and pulled out the picture, setting it on the desk. Then she opened the flat drawer where she kept her pens and pulled out a magnifying glass, which she used to examine the picture.

"It's Ilse. This proves that she was there that night."

She handed me the magnifying glass and picture so I could see for myself. The young woman in the photo had an expression of resolve on her face if I've ever seen one.

"She looks so determined."

"She always did, because she was always up to something."

"How could Ilse be at the lake and at the sleepover at the same time?"

"She must have left the sleepover soon after my mom dropped her off," Bibi said, "not in the middle of the night like everyone thought."

"But how could she be at the lake and running away with Jensen too?"

Bibi pressed her lips together. "I need to ask her. And Lila, I'd like to do this alone, please."

I wanted to insist that I accompany her. It didn't seem fair to cut me out now, when we were so close to figuring out where Ilse had been that night.

On paper, that is. In real life, this was family business and I had no right whatsoever to insert myself into that.

I left quietly as Bibi called Ilse and asked if she would come down to the study.

I wandered into the kitchen. I didn't want to go too far in case Bibi felt inspired to fill me in on her discussion with her sister afterwards, but I'd missed dinner while I read, and if I didn't get some sustenance soon, I might very well be in need of a fainting couch.

After some yogurt and grapes, which was about all I had the energy to scrape together, I cleaned up and turned out the light. I walked through the parlor and had just entered the foyer when a low murmur caught my attention. I followed the sound down the hallway to the great room. The lights were off, but I could see two figures—one very tall and one very small—silhouetted against the far windows. Shrinking back into the hallway, I stood by the corner, listening.

"Not much longer now," a deep voice said.

"Are you sure it will work?" A higher one answered.

"I hope so." It was said in almost a growl.

I peeked around the edge of the wall. Suddenly lights flooded the room and Ilse walked in. "Oh, sorry! Didn't know anyone was in here. I was looking for my bag. I wanted to show Bibi something."

"How is everything going in there?" Alice asked. That was more words than I'd ever heard her utter in a row. "Did you—"

Ilse sighed. "I'm doing my best."

"Thank you for trying," Alice said, crossing the room.

"Anything for you, Auntie," Ilse said, patting her arm.

"Now scoot," Darien said. "Go work your magic."

Ilse left and I stood in the shadows, trying to work out what I'd seen. Show Bibi her bag? Work your magic?

I retreated as quietly as I could and ran up the stairs into the guest room where Ilse was staying. Although I knew she was talking to Bibi, she could come up at any second, so I would have to move fast. I quickly searched the surfaces, looked under the bed, and pulled open drawers. I finally found Ilse's powder-blue hobo bag slumped in the corner between the dresser and the wall. I pawed through it, pulling out her wallet first. Everything looked normal in there—including a license with a California address—so I dumped everything else out onto the ground and examined it. Still looked like basic purse stuff. I picked up the leather bag again and began unzipping pockets. The final interior pocket I checked had a plastic baggie holding a license and a medical card.

With the name Alycia Greenwich.

Chapter 18

I snapped a picture of the cards with my phone and refilled the purse, shoving it back into the corner where I'd found it, then slipped across the hall to my room. I closed the door and enlarged the screen in order examine the photos more closely. Alycia Greenwich lived in California too, but at a different address.

The picture was definitely of the woman who had come to Callahan House this week claiming to be Ilse.

I did a search for Alycia Greenwich on the internet. An address matching the one on the license came up. There were no social media profiles, but there was a link to a grade school class picture posted by a classmate, so it would seem that she had indeed been using that name when she was younger, not just recently. I enlarged it and saved the link.

I went back down to the study and knocked on the open door. Bibi and Ilse were hugging and wiping away tears.

This wasn't going to be pleasant.

"I'm sorry to interrupt, but I need to talk to you, Bibi. It's urgent."

"Of course. Ilse, do you mind?"

"Not at all," Ilse said, patting her sister on the arm and scooting past me.

I held up one finger so Bibi wouldn't say anything. After a

minute, I checked the hallway to ensure that Ilse had left.

"How mysterious," Bibi said, looking intrigued.

"I'm sorry to have to tell you this, but Ilse may not be who she says she is." I held out my phone and tapped it. Bibi scanned the photos of the Alycia Greenwich cards quickly and handed them back.

"Yes, I know that Ilse used a different name."

I gaped at her. "You did?"

"She felt like she had to hide her old self. In order to start over. Jensen apparently changed his name too..."

"To what?"

"I don't know. Probably Mr. Greenwich."

"Speaking of which, did she show you a wedding certificate?"

"What? Goodness no." Bibi laughed. "I don't need one. Who shows other people their wedding certificates?"

"People who are trying to claim an inheritance based on the premise that a wedding took place."

Bibi stared at me. "You think she's trying to get the Callahan money for herself?"

"If she's not Ilse, then yes, I think she may be trying to con you."

"It is Ilse. And I'd *gladly* give my sister half of whatever I have."

"But are you sure? How do you know other than the fact that she showed up here and claimed to be Ilse?"

She frowned. "I think I would recognize my own sister."

"I understand, but look at this..." I pulled up the second-grade class photo and showed Bibi, who examined it carefully.

Finally, she looked up. "The face looks different to me."

"She was much younger," I pointed out. "But if it *is* her, doesn't this show that the timeline is wrong, and that she didn't take on a pseudonym later like she claims?"

Bibi handed back my phone. "Hard to tell. And Lila, that could be someone else with the same name."

I remembered something else. "Tonight, I overheard her talking to the Flemms, and she called Alice 'auntie.'"

"And?"

"I've never heard you call her Aunt Alice."

"But Ilse *did* do that sometimes. It was an honorary title meant to demonstrate her affection. She felt closer to them than I did. Is there anything else? I have work to do." Her tone was frostier than I'd ever heard it before.

"I'm not trying to upset you...I just don't want you to get hurt."

Bibi walked over to the door and opened it. "Thank you for your concern. I believe this conversation is over."

"But—"

"Good night, Lila."

Well, that had been a colossal failure.

If anything, I'd made Bibi feel more protective of Ilse.

I trudged back up to my room, thinking hard. It was late but I knew I wouldn't be able to sleep until I located everything there was to be found about Ilse Smithson Callahan.

I fired up the laptop and did a deep dive, searching for hours.

I was so deep in the zone that when my mother swirled in at one point and asked me what I wanted for Christmas this year, I said, "Answers."

She asked what she had ever done to raise such a philosophical child and whirled away to, presumably, come up with something easier to purchase.

Numerous articles about the Callahans were archived on the *Larkston Live* website. The family was at the core of practically everything Larkston-related, having funded its growth in a variety of ways, not the least of which was selling land that led to the establishment of the town, the college, and numerous parks. They were donors to philanthropic causes, members on school and community boards, and sponsors of cotillion. Larkston definitely had its *haves* and *have nots*; stories often featured the Callahans rubbing elbows with others at the top of the social ladder, like the Shanes and Van Brewers. The passing of each family member was given somber treatment and recorded with dignity, including, for the most part, the mystery surrounding Jamie and Hudson's car accident.

There were far fewer items involving the Smithson family: some inclusion of Bibi and Ilse on honor roll lists, an article about Ilse having won a dance competition, an announcement of Bibi and Jamie's wedding, and, of course, some breathless reporting on Ilse's disappearance, which dwindled rapidly once it became clear that no evidence to explain where she had gone existed.

However, various searches brought up no mention of any Jensen Greenwich. He didn't exist online. No driver's license, voting registration, mortgage, company listing—nothing. I'd have to broach the subject with Bibi, though the way she'd responded earlier made me somewhat wary of bringing it up again. I'd need to approach the topic delicately and thoughtfully.

Nothing had showed up to disprove Ilse's story. Perhaps she was exactly who she said she was, and her husband Jensen had simply chosen a different last name to protest his unhappy relationship with his family. In which case, she was a rightful heir.

And as long as Bibi was comfortable with everything, who was I to say anything about any of it? Maybe it was time for me to take a step backwards.

I gave up and went to bed, where I dreamed again of the Larks at the lake. This time, they were sitting in a circle around the bonfire, just as they had in Bibi's book. There was the sense that something was coming, something unavoidable and dangerous. Then a wave was visible, racing toward us so fast that there was no chance of escape—and when it crested, about to slam down upon us, I awoke, drenched in sweat, shivering.

But I had a new question.

I found Bibi outside on Friday morning, near the light installations. Workers were climbing around the roof, shimmying across the towers, and reaching from ladders to attach the bulbs. Several more were throwing nets over bushes and winding strands around pine trees. Bibi was hanging the adorable partridges she'd made—now painted in shades of red, green, yellow, and blue—around the yard. She saw me coming her way and flinched.

I powered over anyway, inspired by my latest theory. "I'm sorry if I upset you last night. I only wanted to give you the information. Also, I couldn't find any Jensen Greenwich online. For what it's worth."

So much for handling the Jensen thing carefully.

I apologized again.

She smiled at me. "I appreciate that, and I didn't mean to be defensive. Though I do think it would be better if you let go of your investigation for now. I shouldn't have placed that burden on your shoulders in the first place. Please forgive me. I was so distraught about Gillian, and I knew that you had experienced some success in the past with other cases."

I stared at her. "Are you sure?"

"Yes," she said. "I have other responsibilities and so do you." She picked up another partridge and untangled the cord before hanging it on a nearby branch.

"May I ask you a question?"

"Go on."

"When Ilse went missing, did they drag the lake?"

"Of course. Almost immediately."

There went that theory. Oh well.

"Thanks for confirming. It didn't say in the newspaper articles whether they did or not." I surveyed the landscape. "The lights are going to be pretty."

Bibi evaluated her bird placement and adjusted it slightly. "This is my favorite time of year. There's something so peaceful about lights in the dark."

Illumination. There was a worthy goal.

Regardless of what Bibi said, I wasn't walking away from this case. She wasn't paying me, after all, so she couldn't fire me. I did appreciate her realization that sleuthing took time and energy, but I'd woken up more resolved than ever to protect my friend. In addition to finding out what happened to Gillian, I was going to make darn sure that Bibi didn't remain their primary suspect or be conned by Ilse if that was in fact happening.

Whether Bibi realized it or not, she needed assistance.

However, I didn't know what to do next. I'd already shared my suspicions about Ilse, and Bibi hadn't wanted to hear them. I could understand—after all these years of guilt and grief, she had finally gotten her sister back.

Or so she thought.

Remained to be seen.

This was a bit of a pickle. Typically, when I got this tangled up in a problem, I sought advice from Lex. Sadly, he wasn't around.

I wondered when the day would come that I didn't miss him anymore. Months had passed, and it still took powerful resolve not to call his office just to hear his voice on the recorded message.

Don't spiral, I told myself. *He's gone. Accept it and move on.*

I thought for a moment, then picked up my phone and began texting.

Chapter 19

Before long, I was at the diner with Nate and Calista. My mother had begged off, saying she was "feeling inspired by the altitude"—whatever that meant—and wanted to do some sketches for a new piece.

It was lunchtime, so the place was packed. Conversations created a dull roar, punctuated by the clatter of plates and the occasional ding of the bell used to indicate that an order was up. We scored a booth near the back and slid in, wedging our coats in between us. I hadn't been able to stop thinking of the pie since the last time I was here, so I urged them to try it.

"I'm not in the mood for dessert," Calista said.

"But this is no ordinary pie. It's the best pie you'll ever have in your life. It might even be life-changing. I don't know what they put in there, but it's—"

"Delicious?" Nate guessed enthusiastically.

"Way beyond that. Whole other level. You might even say it's magical," I said.

He grinned. "Well, I'm in."

"Me too, I guess," Calista said, unenthusiastically, as a young man in a white shirt and pants arrived, pencil poised over a pad. He jotted down our orders and left.

"I need to bounce something off of you two," I said. "And I need you to promise to keep it to yourselves, please, since it involves someone else."

"Again, you don't need to keep telling us not to say anything. We don't say anything," Calista said. "Ever. You know that."

"I do. But this is a serious and possibly legal situation."

"Well, this sounds even more promising than the magical pie you promised us," Nate said, leaning in.

I filled them in on Ilse, finishing right before the server deposited our coffees and cherry pies on the table. They took a bite and concurred that I hadn't oversold it.

"I might even order a second piece," Nate said. "This is incredible."

"You told Bibi, but she brushed it off?" Calista pulled the creamer jug toward her and poured it.

"Yes. I mean, I sort of understand why she would want to..."

"What makes her so sure that it is her sister?" Nate asked, blowing on his coffee.

"She said she recognizes her. Oh, and Ilse has a tattoo of a dove on her wrist that Bibi said no one else would have known about."

"No one? That's weird." Calista moved her spoon slowly around the mug.

"Ilse got the tattoo the day before she disappeared. And apparently Bibi's mother was so horrified that she excluded it from any descriptions she gave the police."

Nate's eyes widened. "Seems like an important detail."

"Quite," Calista agreed. "Why didn't Bibi tell them?"

"I don't know. She was only eighteen and certainly under duress. Maybe her mother told her not to, and she was scared. Being questioned by the police can be intimidating for anyone."

"Do you think this Ilse is the original Ilse?"

"She may be. Though why would she have identification cards with another name on them? Bibi said Ilse told her that she and

Jensen had wanted a fresh start and that could be true. But if isn't, she's a criminal."

"True." Calista cut into her pie with her fork. I couldn't help noticing that hers was disappearing faster than anyone else's. "Have you asked Ilse directly?"

"I don't want to come right out and ask her yet. If she is up to something, that could scare her away, and I'd rather she be arrested, if that's the case. To prevent future scams."

"What can we do to help?" Nate took a bite of his pie and closed his eyes in delight. "Here for you. And this *pie*."

"Will you come to the Winter Wonderland party and let me know what you think? I can't promise that you'll be able to tell anything at all from seeing Ilse walk around with a cocktail in her hand, but if you stay close to her, perhaps she'll let something slip."

"Winter Wonderland? Is it a costume party?" My cousin's eyes lit up. "I happen to have a very wintry *Game of Thrones* gown that I've been holding onto for just the right moment."

"No, I'm sorry."

"I for one am glad," Nate announced. "My Lovecraft-Monster costume at the conference was a total flop."

Calista turned to him. "What do you mean?"

"I was trying to make a statement, a visible objection to Lovecraft's hateful personal perspectives. I thought if anyone would understand and engage in protest along with me, it was the horror crowd."

"Well, *we* knew what you meant," Calista said. "Probably everyone else did too."

"Or maybe my monster legs weren't *big* enough." Nate frowned. "I should have super-sized them."

"Anyway," I went on, "I could be completely wrong about Ilse...but let's not forget that the Callahans had a lot of money. More than most people will ever see in their lifetime. And money is a potent motivator of bad behavior."

He ran his fork through some whipped cream. "But Bibi told you she'd happily split the money with her sister. So if she wants to do that, it's her business."

"You're right. As long as Ilse *is* her sister. Bibi needs to be able to make an informed decision."

"Have you talked to Lex?" Calista ventured.

"No. I'm talking to you instead." I said it in a tone that meant the matter was closed.

She accepted this with a brief nod. "Then maybe you should mention your theories to the Larkston police."

I laughed. "Detective Ortiz already told me that they weren't interested in hearing them."

"Who cares? Any citizen can march down there and report whatever they want. You don't need to be invited." Nate gave his head an emphatic bob to underscore his point. "And if you want a wingman, I'm your, um, man."

"Do people *need* wingmen for reporting things?" Calista asked doubtfully.

"Just saying," he told her. "Available for all wingman duties, whenever."

That settled, we enjoyed the last morsels of our pie, then debated what enchanted ingredients might be responsible for provoking such bliss.

On my way home, I stopped by the police station. Nate had hyped me up, and I was determined to share my ideas. Detective Ortiz happened to be at the front counter. When I explained that I wanted to share a theory, he asked me to fill out a report. For some reason, seeing the page that he pushed across the counter was maddening.

"I prefer to *tell* you, not fill out a piece of paper that you'll just file away." My gaze fell on the nearby wastebasket. "Perhaps there."

He closed his eyes, summoning the expression of a long-suffering saint. "We follow up on everything, I assure you. Why don't you come back to my desk and I'll type it up as you tell me? Would it make you feel better to see your words go into the computer straightaway?"

"Thank you." The offer did make me feel better, though there was no rational reason why it should. Deleting a file took even less effort than throwing something away.

"Then that's what we'll do."

He led me back to a cubicle. During the short journey, I decided that I didn't *really* believe he would delete my report. Still, it was difficult to shake the feeling that he wouldn't take it seriously, which was prompted wholly by our conversation at the gas station coffee bar when he hadn't wanted to hear anything from me.

Maybe now that I was following formal procedure, he would.

He turned the corner and pointed at our destination, waiting for me to enter first. I sat on the chair next to his desk, which was covered with papers in stacks of different sizes. He had pictures of two boys dressed in baseball uniforms tacked up on the wall. I complimented him on the cute kids, then walked him through my suspicions. At the end, I showed him my photos of the identification cards, which he asked me to email. He didn't comment on my information, just typed diligently and kept his eyes on the computer screen in front of him until I'd finished talking.

"All done?"

"Almost. I'm still wondering whom the police department told about the manuscript?"

"Is that a trick question?" He leaned back in his chair and met my eyes. "The answer is no one."

"How did *Larkston Live* get ahold of the information?"

"I don't know."

"Have you had any problem with leaks in your department?"

The detective frowned.

"Let me ask it another way. How much information typically gets out to the media?"

"It depends. We provide information that we feel is necessary on a case-by-case basis." He moved some papers from one stack to another, then did it again. There didn't seem to be any rhyme or reason to the transfer; he barely glanced at the pages he was handling. It was possible that he was trying to look busy so I would go ahead and leave.

Taking the hint, I went to the heart of my inquiry. "So in this case, someone shared the contents of the manuscript without official approval?"

"Evidently."

"Was it you?"

He scowled. "Of course not."

"Do you know how much of the manuscript was shared? All of it, for example, or selected parts?"

"No idea."

I couldn't gauge his own level of frustration with the leak. As I re-evaluated my approach, he leaned forward and picked up an entire stack of papers. It was a clear indication that he was ready to end this conversation. His eyes scanned the desk, perhaps checking for another item to be added to the pile in his hand.

"You saw the stories on *Larkston Live*, right?"

"I did." He set the pages back down with a small sigh, apparently realizing that I wasn't willing to admit defeat yet.

"So you know the fact that the manuscript was stolen and reappeared was reported, as well as a small bit of the plot itself. That's a lot of information."

"It is."

"And you're saying that the police department did not share that—"

"Officially."

"It could have happened unofficially?"

"It shouldn't have. But sometimes it does."

"Do you think the Throckhams have a mole here?"

He shrugged.

I seemed to have hit a wall.

"Will you please keep an eye out for any wrongdoing?"

"I always do."

I popped up and looked over the dividers to ensure no one was in hearing distance, then lowered my voice. "Bibi is especially concerned that her identity as the author remain private."

"I see." The officer shifted in his seat. "My turn for a question. How did you get ahold of the ID cards in the first place?"

In my retelling, I'd omitted the part about snooping around Ilse's room.

"Let's say I *happened* upon them."

He pressed his lips together as if suppressing a smile. "What do you mean?"

"I mean that I *came upon them* unexpectedly."

He started to speak, but I rattled ahead to prevent having to clarify. "Look, that part doesn't matter. What does matter is that Ilse Callahan is about to inherit half a fortune. It seems like a very small thing to make sure she is who she says she is."

He leaned back and crossed his arms over his chest. "And you think that's a police matter? What about the lawyers who get paid to handle these things? Shouldn't they demand further verification before handing out the money?"

"Yes, but if I don't say anything, they might not. And if I do go to them behind her back, Bibi will be upset with me for meddling in her affairs."

"You aren't already meddling in her affairs?"

That gave me pause, but only for a moment. "I'm trying to look out for her."

"And you don't care if the Larkston police force is upset with you for wasting their time?"

I thought about that for a good long while.

"No," I finally whispered. Might as well be honest.

"All right, then. We're done here." He held his arm out, inviting me to leave. I thanked him for his help. He didn't respond.

That could have gone better.

After I left the police station, I drove to Main Street and parked in the first spot I found along the curb. I wanted to give Bibi a present as thanks for letting me stay at Callahan House. The small shops were decorated for the holidays; there was an abundance of wreaths, ribbons, and pinecones and the scent of cinnamon was somehow in the air.

I wandered into one boutique, where I found some bracelets for my mom and Calista. A display of colorful stained glass panels caught my eye and I asked the owner, who was leafing through a book at the counter, if he happened to have any with larks. He leaped up and ushered me down a long aisle while pointing to various pieces and calling out scientific bird names. While I admired his expertise, it soon felt as though he were reading me the index of a field guide. At the end, he finally located one panel which, he assured me, had a lark in the center. For all I knew, it could have been a North American Lake Hopper or a Plum-Bellied Sparklechaser—those were the kind of sounds he'd been chirping at me, anyway—but the design was beautiful and I hoped Bibi would like it.

Once my purchases had been carefully wrapped, I wandered down the sidewalk, window shopping, until I found myself in front of *Larkston Live*.

Mercy was tapping busily on her keyboard, oblivious to passersby. I couldn't imagine working in such a fishbowl. Sighing, I pushed on the glass door and went inside.

When she recognized me, her mouth tightened.

"Sorry to bother you, Mercy, but I wanted to ask you a quick question, if I may."

"I didn't catch your name the other day."

"Lila Maclean."

"Oh, the professor. My mother told me about you. Come on in." She gestured to a chair at one of the empty desks.

"Thanks. I won't take up much of your time, but I was wondering if you could tell me who has been feeding you information about the manuscript. I've come directly from the police department." I thought I'd work that into the mix, lend an air of authority.

"Directly?" She cast a pointed glance at the shopping bags I was holding.

She had me there. "Almost. Point is, they said they didn't provide any information about the manuscript to *Larkston Live*, but you and your mother have been reporting on it."

She leaned back in her chair and looked me up and down. "You do know how reporting works, don't you? We reporters go after the stories. We find sources. We ask questions. We don't rest until we uncover the truth." It was clear that she valued heroic pluck. I did too.

"And you have a tip line."

Her face fell. "That's one of the ways we launch our investigations, yes," she said stiffly.

"How many calls do you receive a week?"

"I'm not at liberty to give out that information, but it's not a huge number or anything."

It was interesting how Tacey crowed about her tip line and said her phone was constantly ringing off the hook, but Mercy didn't seem to want to acknowledge it.

I waited for her to expand on her answer, which she didn't do. "Did the manuscript information come from the tip line? Or did someone from the police department share it with you?"

Mercy reached for the mug on her desk and took a sip. "Are you accusing the Larkston police of leaking the story?"

"No. I'm trying to figure out what happened. As I said, I already spoke to the police."

She laughed. "I bet they *loved* that."

I persisted. "Do you have a contact in the police department who fed it to you?"

"Please. If someone there was feeding me stories, they wouldn't last long on the force. It would be too easy for the brass to figure out."

"So the information about the manuscript *did* come from the tip line?"

"I'm under no obligation to tell you anything." Mercy sighed. "Now, if that's all you wanted to know, do you think I might return to my work?"

Not telling me in this case felt a lot like telling me. Who had left the tip? And why?

I thanked her for her time and turned to go.

"Feel free to stop by any time," she warbled before the door closed.

I do not think she meant it.

After crossing the street carefully, I loaded my packages into the trunk of the car. I needed to get home, change, and head over to the college campus. As if she didn't have enough to do, Bibi had taken it upon herself to ensure that a memorial service for Gillian was scheduled as quickly as possible. I had offered to help, but she said that the Larks would take care of everything.

It was starting to get dark, and the cold temperatures would soon solidify the ice that had liquefied into slush during the day. I drove slowly and carefully, especially over the bridge. The top layer of ice on the lake had melted in places, creating gaps where dark water was visible underneath. An intense uneasiness descended, surely due to the memory of my dreams. They were some of the most vivid I'd ever had. I knew my subconscious was trying to tell me something. But what?

My phone trilled, startling me so much that I almost hit the ceiling with my head. It was a number I didn't recognize, but I pushed the speaker button anyway. I welcomed any distraction from the trepidation flowing through me, even if it came from a telemarketer.

"Dr. Maclean?" The chancellor's cultured voice filled my car.

Immediately, I regretted my choice. "Yes?"

"Trawley Wellington here." Sometimes he said his name like that to sound like an everyday guy, but you were supposed to call him "chancellor" in return, make no mistake. I'd seen him pointedly refer to himself by title if someone didn't use it the first time they spoke to him.

"How are you, Chancellor?"

"Fine, fine. Listen, I wanted to check in on Callahan House. Did you have a chance to talk to Bibi?"

No, I had not pleaded the chancellor's case, as he had urged me to do. Once he had raised the question of tenure next to the request to speak to Bibi on his behalf, I couldn't do it. He hadn't stated anything outright, but I wasn't comfortable with the proximity of topics.

Explaining that to him, however, was unthinkable. There was

no conceivable positive outcome: he'd either be furious that I was refusing to do his bidding or outraged that I was accusing him of extortion. Maybe there were additional equally horrible options, but two was more than enough.

"Dr. Maclean?"

I tried desperately to come up with a response, but I couldn't think of anything to say. Eventually, I made a small sound that was supposed to be a noncommittal murmur but came out like a cross between a hum and a meow.

Instant mortification.

He didn't say anything. Maybe he hadn't heard that.

Was that a faint chuckle, or merely the wind blowing tumbleweeds over the ghost town where my dignity lived?

Then his voice boomed so loudly that my windows rattled. "*Are you still there*? *Is this a bad connection?*"

"Yes, sorry. I'm...on the bridge." What was I even saying? The bridge had perfect reception. He'd lived in this town and undoubtedly knew that.

I gripped the steering wheel tightly.

The next time he spoke, his volume was lower, but his level of intensity remained the same. "Well, Dr. Maclean? Did you talk to Bibi about the sale?"

"I did talk to Bibi about the sale." There. That was actually true. The chancellor's name had not been part of that conversation, but I wasn't claiming that it had been.

"What can you tell me about my chances?"

That was trickier territory. I aimed for broad strokes. "I think she may have another offer, but I don't know for sure if she's selling." I didn't think I should mention that Ilse could have a stake in the sale. It wasn't my news.

"Find out, will you?"

"What? I can't hear you, Chancellor. Are we still connected?" I made a crackling sound in my throat, then hung up fast, before he thought I had agreed to do anything else that I didn't want to do.

My phone rang again immediately afterwards, but I ignored it.

Chapter 20

By the time I arrived at the campus chapel, it was full. I took one of the programs from a student usher and slipped into the back row. The sconces along the walls were dim, but the colorful windows glowed, backlit by an unseen illumination system. Large bouquets of white roses were positioned on either side of the pulpit, and a screen above flashed pictures of Gillian at regular intervals—standing with friends, sitting in classrooms, walking her dog, leading protests, graduating from college, marrying Hudson, cutting the ribbon on her agency doors, hiking in the mountains, accepting awards, and so on. In all of them, her wide smile lit up her face, and she was often laughing with the family and friends surrounding her.

"Welcome, everyone. Thank you for coming. We're here to remember and celebrate the life of Gillian Elizabeth Shane." Bibi spoke at length, painting a picture of a treasured friend and beloved member of the Larkston community. Each of the Larks went up to speak, as did Winston and Hudson, followed by a number of co-workers and individuals from the town. They highlighted her exceptional kindness, humor, and willingness to help others. Their tributes were extremely moving—there wasn't a dry eye in the house, including mine. A string quartet played "The Long and Winding Road," then an acapella choir from the college sang "Somewhere Over the Rainbow." Weeping could be heard around the room during both performances.

Afterwards, Bibi invited us all to the student union for a potluck dinner. On my way out of the chapel, I noticed the tables that had been set up at the end of the narthex, where people had stored their food during the service. I'd missed them on the way in, but now mourners were gathering their pots and pans for the walk across campus.

We moved as a group along the snowy sidewalks. The cold was almost unbearable, but the skies were clear and full of stars. In general, the crowd was subdued, which was to be expected given the reason for the gathering, but there were momentary bursts of chatter. After we'd filed into the doors of the union, the group broke apart—some heading to the area where food was to be set up, others moving toward seats at the circular atrium tables.

Bibi caught me by the elbow and asked me to help her with the items that needed heating. I made several trips into the kitchen, delivering items to the people working the ovens and microwaves, and carrying warm dishes back to the tables. Once that was done, Margot clapped her hands to get everyone's attention and invited them to help themselves. As people began to assemble in a line, my phone chirped with a notification, which turned out to be a new post from *Larkston Live*: "Bibi Callahan and Margot Van Brewer: Model Citizens or Murderers?"

People started checking their phones, reacting with surprise, and turning to look at the two women. Conversations began to swell and there was an electric energy in the room. Margot glanced at her screen, then showed it to Bibi, whose eyes widened. They scrolled through the post, conferred with one another, then marched over to Mercy Throckham, who was standing near the front doors with an unmistakably smug expression. She wore an orange coat that matched her hair and stood out among the sea of us clad in black.

I couldn't hear what Margot was saying, but her wild

gesticulations suggested that it wasn't a calm conversation. Understandable, really, after being accused of murder at a potluck dinner attended by the whole town.

I hurried over, as did a number of other guests. Penelope coasted to a stop next to me. Soon, a circle had formed around the trio.

"How dare you, Mercy!" Margot's face was almost as red as her hair. "Dragging our good names through the mud on this of all nights, when we're trying to honor our friend."

Mercy's hands clenched into fists. "How dare *you*? Have you forgotten that my mother is dead too? Why didn't you include her in your little party?"

"It's a memorial, not a *party*," Margot hissed. "What is wrong with you?"

"Wait," Bibi said, putting her hand out toward Mercy. "Are you upset that we didn't include Tacey, or are you upset because you think we had something to do with your mother's passing?"

Mercy's eyeballs moved back and forth sideways while she processed the options. "Both, actually."

"I'm very sorry you feel that way. But Gillian doesn't have any close family left, so it was up to us to do something in her memory—"

"And it's up to *you*, Mercy," Margot interjected, "to do something for your own mother. Why would we do that? She wasn't our friend. In fact, she did everything in her power to tear down our reputations with her silly posts and outright lies. Just like you're doing now."

"Is that why you killed her?" Mercy yelled at Margot, taking a step forward. "Am I next?"

I started to move, but Penelope put her hand on my arm. "Let them sort it out," she said in a low voice. "This has been a long time coming."

"We didn't do anything," Margot said.

"Oh, you didn't get questioned by the police?" Mercy asked, cocking her head.

"That doesn't mean we had anything whatsoever to do with murder," Margot retorted. "You have no right to suggest that it does."

"That's exactly what it means," Mercy shot back.

"Haven't you ever heard of police speaking to witnesses in order to investigate leads? Not everyone they talk to is a suspect. Do you know *nothing* about how the world works?" Margot snapped.

"I report what I hear," Mercy protested. "You two were questioned. The town has a right to know."

"And we have the right to sue you for libel," Margot said.

Mercy smirked. "Aren't you forgetting a little something called the First Amendment?"

"And aren't you forgetting a little something called telling the *truth*?" Margot threw her hands up in the air.

"I'm a journalist." Mercy stamped her foot.

"You're an idiot," Margot replied. "Maybe you should try *facts* next time."

"What's going on here?" Winston cut through the crowd.

"Mercy is accusing us of murder," Margot informed him.

"Not to mention ruining the potluck," Penelope said to me quietly.

"Might I have a word with you, Ms. Throckham?" The president's strained smile wavered slightly.

"Fine," she said, allowing him to steer her away but pausing to deliver one more blast over her shoulder. "Everything will be known, Margot. Count on *that*."

Bibi and Margot huddled together. Penelope asked me to help her steer everyone back to the food line, which I did, then we rejoined the Larks.

"Well," Margot said, smoothing her hair. "That was invigorating."

Bibi's eyes were blazing. "She can't really believe what she wrote, can she? That we're murderers?"

"Who knows? Both of the Throckhams are cut from the same cloth...a bolt of stupidity." Margot's smile was tight.

"I hope she takes the post down soon," Penelope said. "But don't worry. No one believes her."

"I'm not so sure about that." Bibi tilted her head toward the food tables.

I surveyed the room. People were in fact darting uneasy glances in our direction from all over the atrium.

"Well, heck. *We* know we didn't do it," Margot said. "Let's carry on with our heads held high. For Gillian."

"For Gillian," Bibi echoed.

"And besides," Margot went on, "our lawyers will have a field day with this. We've been wanting take action against *Larkston Live* for a long time. They have transformed our local newspaper into a nasty gossip blog. It's extraordinarily harmful for our community. Winston was reluctant to move forward because he thought it might cause unpleasantness for the college, but now we can hardly sit back and do nothing. She attacked us. Her allegations are serious. Maybe we can get the site shut down once and for all."

Bibi didn't respond.

"Oh, and don't tell anyone about that plan, of course," Margot said, patting her heart twice. The others followed suit.

"You too, Lila," Margot urged. "You know all our secrets now. In fact, we should probably go ahead and make you a Lark."

"Second that," Bibi said.

"Agreed," Penelope added.

"Perfect. Lila, you're an honorary Lark. Make the pledge of

secrecy, please." Margot patted her heart twice and gestured for me to do the same.

I did it, feeling a little foolish.

"Good," Margot said. "Time to circulate. Chin up, sisters."

Later that night, I couldn't sleep. Why would Mercy accuse Margot and Bibi of murder? Was it as straightforward as the fact that they'd been questioned a second time, after the night Gillian was killed, and the others hadn't? Or was there something more?

Based on our previous conversations, I knew Mercy wouldn't be willing to explain anything to me directly. I'd have to ponder what I already knew.

It was difficult to consider Bibi, whom I viewed as a glorious and admirable human in every way, as a suspect, but I needed to set aside my bias for a moment and think carefully through the possibilities. *Was* there any conceivable reason that Bibi would have wanted Gillian or Tacey dead?

Aside from the fact, as Margot had pointed out, that Tacey posted hurtful things about them whenever she felt like it. That was something, I supposed.

I thought back to Tacey's comment at the diner the day I met her about how Margot had bossed everyone around in high school. It wasn't hard to imagine her as Queen Bee. Someone else had described Margot and Winston as the golden couple. And the Larks probably had seemed like a clique to everyone else.

Those feelings could run deep.

And there certainly wasn't any love lost between Margot and Tacey.

However, Bibi hadn't seemed overtly antagonistic to Tacey, even if Margot had.

But what about Gillian? What if Bibi caught her in the library with the manuscript? What if Gillian had enthused about publishing it and Bibi, desperate to prevent that, had stopped her the only way she knew how?

No. That didn't make any sense. Bibi would have had to sign a contract with Gillian giving her permission as an agent to shop the manuscript around to publishers. Then there would have needed to be another signed contract giving the publisher the rights to put out the book. Bibi knew all that, as an author.

Could it have been something else, something personal? And had Bibi put me on the case to make it seem like she was trying to solve the mystery but actually to point suspicion away from herself?

I turned over to my side, readjusting the pillow.

No matter how hard I tried, I could *not* imagine Bibi murdering anyone. In my bones, I didn't believe she was capable of anything so heinous. Plus, Bibi had been in full sight of everyone at the book club. She didn't have a chance to sneak away and strangle anyone.

Then again, what reason would Margot have had for killing Gillian? Or Penelope or Ilse, for that matter? None that I could think of. As for the husbands—they all seemed to admire Gillian too, from what I could tell.

Was I looking at this from the wrong angle? My thoughts went round and round.

Maybe the second murder was done by a completely different person.

Maybe it was only a copycat of the first.

Maybe the two murders weren't related at all.

Or maybe the only way they made sense *was* to consider them together.

I flipped back and stared at the ceiling. All I knew for sure was that someone in Larkston was lying to the rest of us.

Chapter 21

Committee members descended like an army of ants on Saturday morning and transformed the quiet mansion into an energetic stream of activity. For most of the day, they were cleaning, moving furniture, organizing food, testing the sound system, and gathering in clumps here, there, and everywhere. An hour before the party began, they went home to change, though the caterers were still racing around doing their thing.

I dressed for the event in my usual black shirt and pants, adding a long velvet jacket that I'd found in a vintage shop a few years ago and had never worn. Dark, with a red and green floral design embroidered down the front and around the hem, it seemed especially festive—and I wanted to wear something special since this marked the end of my stay at Callahan House. After braiding my hair, I added some dangling scroll earrings with a vaguely Victorian style, which seemed appropriate for the setting.

Bibi met me on the stairs.

"Oh, don't you look exquisite, Lila!" she exclaimed, beaming at me. "Happy holidays, dear, if I haven't mentioned it yet."

"Thank you, and happy holidays to you as well. And—"

"Don't say a word about my clothes, please. I decided to repot some poinsettias for the porch at the last minute, and it was messier than I'd thought it would be." She wiped her forehead with her arm, leaving a dirt smear. "Would you mind doing a final walkthrough? I think we've gotten everything done, but I've run out of time and would like to freshen up before any guests arrive."

I agreed and started with the great room, which had been transformed. All the usual seating had been removed to make space for tall round tables with white tablecloths, so that people could have a place to set their plates. The tables would be whisked away after people ate to create a dance floor. The deejay was already in the corner opposite the large tree, playing classical music. White crystal lights had been suspended at varying lengths from the ceiling, so it looked as if snowflakes were descending. The result was breathtaking.

Next, I checked the library, which had taken in furniture from the great room to create a lounge area, with sofas and chairs arranged in conversational groupings. Along the windows, three bartenders stood behind a table with drink fixings at the ready. A separate table on the right held a self-serve punch bowl and a chocolate fountain with an empty platter—I guessed the fruit was forthcoming—and a bowl of candy canes. Seeing that everything was in order there, I went to the parlor, where the caterers had set up tables for the buffet against the front wall. A row of steaming silver chafer sets had cards with calligraphy identifying the contents, and a perpendicular station at the end held an arrangement of multi-tiered dessert towers. In the corner between the two, there was a square table with only a lace tablecloth on it.

Bibi appeared. She had changed into a long green dress with a shimmering bodice. Her hair was up in an elegant twist, which showed off her emerald dangle earrings that sparkled in the light.

"You look beautiful, Bibi."

She thanked me and asked how everything was going.

"Everything looks ready except..." I pointed at the empty table.

"Oh, that's for the centerpiece in case Brody—"

"I did," came a voice from behind us. We turned around to see

Brody, holding a cooler, standing in the foyer.

"You made it!" Bibi laughed. "I wasn't sure you remembered our bet."

"Of course I did," he grumbled, though it was genial. "And I hope this will suffice. Where does it go?"

Bibi opened the door all the way—"so that guests can come on in"—and led him over to the table in the corner of the parlor. "How's this?"

"That'll work." He set the cooler down and reached inside. First, he removed a square metal tray with upturned edges and set it on the table. Then he went back to the cooler and pulled out a bag of polished black rocks, which he poured into the tray. He bent down and lifted out something else, setting it carefully on top of the stones. He arranged the rocks at the base more precisely, then took a step back and made a ta-da gesture with his hands.

It was a two-foot-tall ice sculpture of Callahan House. Brody had captured every quirky architectural detail.

Bibi clutched his arm while we gushed over his art for several minutes. He blushed and shuffled his feet for the duration and was visibly relieved when she led him over to the bar. I moved around the table, taking pictures from different angles to send to Bibi later. Something about the sculpture triggered the sense of an idea at the back of my mind, but I couldn't quite grasp it yet.

"What a fine replica." The chancellor was standing beside me. "Who's the artist? I'd like to commend them."

"Brody Salton. He's here now. Would you like me to introduce you? Come this way." I started walking, hoping that a quick jaunt across the lobby and into the library would be all that was required of this conversation.

"Wait, I'd like to have a word first." He offered me a smile, something so rare and unnerving that I broke out in goosebumps. "Here we are, standing before Callahan House in miniature. Very symbolic, wouldn't you say?" The chancellor had once been an English professor, which emerged in unexpected ways. I didn't know if he found symbolism in the fact that the sculpture replicated the house he wanted to buy or in the fact that the sculpture was much smaller than his large powerful presence, but if he found symbolism in the moment, who was I to argue?

I smiled back at him.

He returned his gaze to the ice sculpture. "Do you have any news for me? I haven't heard back from Bibi, and I'm concerned."

That was one discussion I didn't want to be part of. "Would you like me to get her for you? You can speak to her right now. She may still be with Brody, the artist, which would be a happy case of two birds, one—"

"No. There's a strategy to this, Dr. Maclean. If I seem too eager, she'll raise the price."

"Right now, you don't even know if she is considering your offer at all, though."

The chancellor narrowed his eyes. "I thought you said she was."

"I did not say—"

He cut me off with a long sigh. "*Do* take me to find her. Please."

I led him into the library, where Bibi and Brody were in fact together, and made introductions. Before I left, the chancellor twisted around, lowered his chin and his voice, and reminded me that he was counting on me. Then he turned back to the conversation with a wide smile and launched his charm offensive. I sighed in relief and went over to the bar, where I requested a cabernet sauvignon with ice. The last part made a muscle in the bartender's cheek twitch, but he didn't comment. I tipped him and took my drink out into the foyer, where guests had begun streaming in, so I quickly rerouted and went into the great room.

Penelope was standing at one of the tables, looking up at the snowflake lights, which had been switched on. The soft glow made the effect even more striking.

"Wow," she breathed. "That's the first time they've done the lights that way. I feel like I'm in a fairy tale. Bibi pulled out all the stops."

"And the committee members—I can't believe how many people chipped in. How many are there?"

She moved closer, the gold threads in her taupe sheath catching the light. "I don't know. Countless people. I feel almost guilty about my own small contribution."

"Why?" I took a sip of my wine, which was delicious.

"Choosing the caterer is—don't tell—the absolutely best job. You get to taste all of the food, and once you've made your choice, the caterers do the rest." Penelope chuckled. "Help on the front end is my enduring strategy."

"Genius. I'll have to keep that in mind. By the way, Brody's sculpture is incredible. How long did it take him to make it?"

She looked up at the lights above and smiled. "A long time."

"Why did he decide to use ice instead of clay?"

"I don't think he wanted the commemoration to last. He has mixed feelings about Callahan House."

"What do you mean?"

"We have so many memories here. They're mostly good, but at times, things have felt a bit clique-ish."

"With whom?"

"Just between us, okay?" When I affirmed, she continued. "Jamie, Hudson, Gillian, Margot, and Winston came from money; Bibi, Brody, and I didn't. Sometimes it felt like they were rubbing it in our faces, though they weren't doing it intentionally. Bibi navigated it much more gracefully than we did, I'm afraid. I never heard her mention it once."

"Did that ever cause any problems among the group members?"

She tipped her head to the side, thinking. "Hudson was the only one who mentioned it overtly. He was pretentious, and he could be a bully. Those two things never go well together. Sometimes he would try and goad others into getting into arguments with him, but it was mostly when he had too much to drink. The rest of the time, he was fine. We were very fond of him, of course."

"Fond of whom? Me?" A tuxedo-clad Winston threw his arms over both of our shoulders, jostling us. He laughed.

I glanced down at the front of my jacket, but I couldn't tell if I was wearing a wine stain or not. It was one upside of wearing black, despite my mother's ongoing campaign to rotate brighter colors into the mix. Cheers to that.

"Ignore him," Margot commanded, gliding up to Penelope. Her off-the-shoulder red gown smoldered even in the dim light. "And good evening to you."

We exchanged greetings and complimented each other's finery, then they all trotted off to the bar in the library. I was glad to have a moment to myself, to process what Penelope had told me. She'd confirmed what Bibi had said about Hudson's tendency to become more aggressive with alcohol. Since she'd been in a sharing mood, I should have pressed her about the rumors that had circulated about Jamie and Ilse before Winston and Margot showed up. There hadn't been anything in Bibi's book about those—was she trying to protect her sister or her boyfriend? It was such a tangled web, those friendships.

Bibi appeared in the great room and rang a bell, inviting us to the parlor buffet. People eagerly moved in that direction. I went upstairs instead to check on my mother. I was surprised that she hadn't come down yet. When I knocked on her bedroom door, she called for me to come in.

She was still in her robe, applying makeup. "Darling, hello. I know I'm running a bit late, but Daphne called and told me the most astounding things about an article that's going to run in the *Times* about my latest work."

She'd been working on "Skirts" for over a year—an exhibit at a trendy new gallery that featured one of her persevering themes: *femmes fatales*. From what I could gather, it was a combination of mannequins made out of lipstick tubes and bullet shells, draped with fabrics that flowed far beyond the body to form ominous towering shapes of their own. As was often the case in recent years, she had incorporated multimedia clips, so that faces of iconic noir actresses glided over everything while film scores played in the background.

"Good things in the article?"

"Wonderful things. I'll tell you later. How's the party?"

"It's happening. Will you be coming down soon?"

"I wouldn't miss it. Though I'm afraid I didn't know I'd be attending such an elegant affair, so I'll have to make do with what I have. It's not a day dress, but..." She opened her suitcase and pulled out a gown that almost blinded me. It looked like it was made of a million diamonds. She could have worn it to the Oscars and blended right in.

Maybe she had.

It was shocking, almost, how much my mother's lifestyle had changed after becoming a famous artist. She may dress in designer clothes and live in a New York City brownstone now, but Calista, Mom, and I were always moving around the country when I was growing up. From art colony to teaching job to who knows where, Violet O had flitted from gig to gig like a jubilant butterfly. Back then, she wore flip flops and jeans, had colorful smears all over her clothes, and walked around with paintbrushes or pencils sticking out of her hair.

"That's a stunning gown, Mom." No wonder her bag had weighed so much. It had been full of stones.

At that thought, I snapped my fingers.

She looked at me questioningly.

"I need to make a call—I'll see you downstairs."

"Ta ta, darling," she called after me.

I went into my room, closed the door, dug the card Detective Ortiz had given me out of my bag, and dialed.

Shortly afterwards, my mother made a grand entrance on the landing—the crowd responded as if spotlights were aimed at her—and immediately bonded with Margot, who had no doubt been drawn to Violet by the undeniable splendor of her dress. After exchanging designer information and stories, Margot spent the rest of the night introducing her around.

After a few hours, it felt like we'd been at the party for days. The guests had eaten delicious food and transitioned into dancing mode. My colleagues had fulfilled their promise to show up, and they appeared both festive and formal—Calista in a fancy golden frock with a wide black velvet belt and Nate in a charcoal gray suit with a red shirt. He'd even gathered his sun-streaked hair back into a small ponytail. I was ecstatic to see that Francisco was with them, looking handsome as ever. He had paired his dark suit with a bow tie the same color as Calista's dress.

"All three of you are gorgeous," I said, after hugging them.

"I feel like I'm being dragged to a prom," Francisco protested. "This bow tie was her idea."

She elbowed him. "We look adorable, babe. Deal with it."

I congratulated him on finishing his book on Flynn McMaster, who had been the keynote speaker at an ill-fated conference that

Nate, Calista, and I had attended.

"It's brilliant," Nate said. "He let me proofread it."

Francisco adjusted his glasses with an air of embarrassment. "Thanks, Nate. And congratulations to you as well, Lila. I heard you finished your book too."

"We need to toast the two of you," Nate said. "Where's the bar?"

"Nice ponytail, by the way," Francisco said to him. "Copying me?"

Nate looked at Francisco's shoulder-length dreadlocks, which were pulled back at the moment. "Well, you *are* magnificent."

"Don't I know it," Calista said, looping her arm through Francisco's.

He kissed the top of her head, then turned back to me. "The important thing is that now we can rejoin the rest of the world. At least until we start another project."

"What are you going to focus on now?"

"Working something up," he said mysteriously.

No matter how hard we pressed him, he wouldn't say anything more.

"Should we get those drinks?" Calista asked.

I held up my wine.

Francisco and Calista walked away, arm in arm.

Nate reached back and fiddled with the ponytail fastener. "Not sure I'm pulling this off."

"You are. It's very cool."

"Not as cool as a man bun—" He stopped, then grinned at me. "Would you believe that Fran wrote an entire book on Flynn McMaster and didn't mention the man bun *once*?"

"He wasn't at the conference with us," I reminded him. "He didn't see it in all its glory."

"That's true. It was a sight to behold."

"It was unforgettable."

He chuckled as he loped away to catch up with Calista and Francisco.

The chancellor caught my colleagues in the hallway, inquiring loudly whether all of their final grades had been submitted by the deadline. They assured him that they'd indeed done their job and continued on to the bar.

Much to my dismay, the chancellor pivoted and made a beeline for me.

"I had a very informative talk with Dr. Callahan." Like Winston, he was wearing a tuxedo. I'd have put money on the fact that neither one had rented them. I might have even taken a bet that they had more than one tuxedo in their closets.

"Ah." I was regretting that the drink in my hand prevented me from having an excuse to go along with my friends.

"You didn't tell me that there may be an issue with the sale in the first place...involving a long-lost sister?" He looked down his nose, then leaned in. "What do you know about that?"

As I was presented with one of his smug expressions for the billionth time, something flared up inside me. "I'm sorry, Chancellor, but I don't feel comfortable talking about Bibi's business. I can't help you."

His eyebrows almost disappeared into his hairline.

I shrugged and smiled at him.

Not at all apologetically.

His mouth flapped open and closed a few times before he settled on an old standby. "I'm disappointed in you, Dr. Maclean."

I watched him walk away, registering a mix of emotions. Yes, I was tired of him pushing me around, but it was very possible that I'd just blown my whole career.

I don't know what came over me.

Exasperation, mostly.

Though that didn't pay the rent.

Resolving not to panic—at least tonight—I wandered into the great room, which was full of bodies flailing around to the beat. When the deejay switched to a slow song, the people on the floor reconfigured themselves into couples.

"Care to dance?" Nate asked, tapping me on the shoulder. "The line for the bar was too long, so we thought we'd dance first."

"Sure." I set my glass on a nearby table.

He put his palm out, and when I placed my hand in his, led me onto the floor. Usually when I agreed to slow dance with someone, they pulled me in too closely and I spent the entire time cataloging all the ways in which it was awkward and hoping the song would hurry up and end. With Nate, though, it was comfortable. He clasped one of my hands and rested his other one lightly on my back. We could have passed muster at any waltz academy.

"Do you have anything to report yet?" I asked, looking up at him. "Ilse-wise?"

He frowned. "Not much. We've only had one Ilse sighting so far, and she behaved herself perfectly. Sorry to disappoint."

"It was a long shot," I replied. "What are the odds she'd do something incriminating in the middle of a holiday party, anyway?"

"Agree. It would be *much* easier if she would just confess that she's up to something." He spun me around in a circle. "Lay out the scheme for us."

"My suspicions may not be warranted," I said. "There's always that."

Nate shook his head. "I trust your sleuthing instincts. And regardless of the outcome, I am happy to have the opportunity to be your sidekick once again."

"I'm forever grateful." I patted his shoulder.

"Remember when I tried to save you that first time, and I got there too late?"

We laughed.

"You are a most excellent sidekick," I assured him. "Hope I can return the favor someday."

"You already have," he said. "We are each other's sidekicks. Well, Calista, too. We are a triangle of sidekicks."

I raised an eyebrow. "That's...not a thing."

Nate looked over my head, thinking. "A crimefighting *trio*?"

"Sure."

"Actually, make that a quartet because there's Fran too." He dipped me.

"Yes! Though aren't those terms used to refer mostly to groups of musicians? I could be wrong."

"A tetrad, then?" He steered us around a couple that had stopped in our path to indulge in some enthusiastic PDA.

"And we can't forget Tad." My next-door neighbor traveled a lot with his boyfriend, but when he was around, he wholeheartedly jumped into the fray.

"So," he squinted at the ceiling, "we're up to a quintet? I mean, a quintuplet? Maybe we should go with something like gang or crew, to take the math out of it."

"Sounds good."

"As long as you know that I'm your most devoted sidekick, that's what matters."

"You're seeking top billing, in other words?" I teased him.

"That's it, in a nutshell. I want my name on the marquee." He twirled me around again.

"Duly noted." I came back to him slightly off-balance and grabbed his bicep by mistake. Surprisingly solid.

"Oops," I said, replacing my hand on his shoulder.

"So are you ready to come back to Stonedale?" He moved his hand from my back to my waist. "Because it's not the same—"

"Sorry to interrupt, but I have some news," Calista said,

waving her hand in between us to display a glittering square diamond on a thick silver band. We yelped in surprise and pulled Calista and Francisco in for a group hug.

"When? How?" I asked her, when we finally broke apart.

"Just now by the Christmas tree," she said, her eyes shining. "So romantic."

Francisco was beaming.

"Is *this* the secret project you were working on and wouldn't tell us about?" I asked.

"It is," he said, straightening his bow tie. "I have been carrying this ring around for months. Nowhere ever seemed special enough."

"This was perfect," my cousin told him.

He kissed her.

Calista took his hand. "We'd be thrilled if you would be our maid of honor and best man."

"I've always wanted to be a maid of honor," said Nate.

She giggled.

"Just kidding. I would never step on Lila's toes," he declared. "Unless we're dancing. Then anything could happen."

"Already did," I said, pointing to my shoes.

Calista tried again. "Will you two—?"

Nate and I said yes simultaneously, congratulated them a thousand times, and raced to the bar to find some champagne.

We'd gone upstairs so the betrothed couple could share their news with my mother when Bibi came to the door. Violet explained what we were celebrating, and she joined us for more merriment. We toasted them profusely, talked about potential wedding venues, and took a barrage of pictures.

After a little while, she pulled me aside. "The caterer said that someone's waiting for you in the study, Lila."

I followed her downstairs. In the foyer, she paused. "I don't know why I'm leading you. You know where the study is. Do you mind if you take yourself the rest of the way?"

I laughed. "Who's in there?"

"I have no idea. I was in the kitchen when I received word. Do you want me to accompany you?"

"No, that's fine. Thanks for telling me." I hoped it was Detective Ortiz following up on my call.

Bibi wiggled her fingers at me and headed back to the kitchen.

I made my way to the study and pushed open the door.

Then I stopped in my tracks.

It was a detective, but not the one I expected.

Lex Archer leaned against the desk holding a bouquet of red lilies. He started talking rapidly, as if he expected me to whirl around and leave at the sight of him.

Which was a good idea because I *had* been about to whirl around and leave at the sight of him.

"Lila, please listen. I know you think Helena and I are together. What you *don't* know is that I only went to Seattle with her because she told me she wanted to live out her final days there. She loves the city. We weren't a couple, *not* at all"—he paused to allow that to sink in—"but I couldn't let her die alone. No one deserves that."

"No one does. You're right about that, and I'm sorry to hear about Helena."

He waited as if he expected me to say more. He eased away from the desk and stood in front of me, the flowers hanging down by his side.

"But why didn't you tell me, Lex?"

"I gave her my word. And I did try to reach out to you—"

"You wouldn't have told me what was really going on. You just *said* that she swore you to secrecy." Heat spread through my chest.

"That's true, but at least we could have talked through it..." He shook his head. "You're right. I don't know what I would have said. But it wouldn't have just been this...silence."

I glared at him. "Here's the thing, Lex. You told me that night at Tattered Star Ranch that there would be no more secrets between us. Ever."

His eyes locked on mine. "I know I did. This involved extreme circumstances. But here's the important thing: I just found out that she was *lying*. The whole time. It was a complete charade to avoid the divorce."

I remembered the day he filed for divorce as if it were yesterday. We'd been so happy. Helena hadn't wedged herself completely between us yet.

"Lila, when I learned the truth, I caught the next flight out of there...and you better believe that the divorce is back on. I'm so sorry."

Were those tears in his eyes? Or was it a trick of the light?

He held out the lilies. "Please forgive me. I've missed you, Professor."

"I've missed you too, Detective."

But I didn't take the flowers.

I didn't move at all.

Although I'd dreamed about reuniting with him for months, I had a powerful revelation: if I were still in love with Lex, I would be in his arms right now.

And I wasn't.

He took a step forward. "Do you need some time? I understand. I'll give you as much time as you need."

"It's not that," I said, slowly. I needed someone I could trust with my heart. That was no longer possible with Lex. No matter what he said or did, there would be a question in the back of my mind.

"You believe me, right? About Helena lying?"

"I do." I looked into his eyes. "You're a good man, Lex. But it's over between us."

His face turned to stone.

There was nothing else to say.

This night had been an emotional roller coaster. I took stock while I helped the caterers pack up. I was beyond thrilled for Calista and Francisco, of course, and I was relieved that Lex and I had achieved some sort of closure. It surprised me to realize that I didn't feel anything other than nostalgia for what we had once had. The anger and hurt I'd been carrying around had completely dissipated. Our time apart must have smoothed away the edges, without me noticing.

Odd how that happens.

The house gradually emptied, and Bibi came in to tell me that the Larks would be staying until the end, which was their tradition. She invited me to join them for a nightcap, then she went off to find them. I kept checking my phone, hoping Detective Ortiz would return my call, but it remained silent. Eventually, I wandered into the parlor, where everything had been removed except Brody's sculpture, which was now a sad, rounded lump sticking out of the rocks.

As I stared at the ice, Calista and Francisco called me from the foyer. She apologized for not having gathered any useful evidence regarding Ilse.

"Are you kidding? Who cares? You're engaged!"

She smiled happily. "We have phone calls to make, so we're leaving. Talk soon?"

"Yes."

"Bye, Aunt Vi," she said, and my mother blew her a kiss. She had been sitting on the stairs texting someone—probably her best frenemy Daphne to humblebrag about what a hit her dress had been. They did that type of thing a lot. Or perhaps she was circulating Calista and Francisco's engagement news among her group of friends back home.

"Have a wonderful night. Love you." I walked Francisco and Calista to the front door, admired her ring again, hugged them once more, and sent them on their way. When I turned around, Nate was walking toward me.

"Hey, maid of honor."

"Hey, best man."

He had almost reached me when Patsy Wellington rushed out of the library, wringing her hands.

"Are you all right?" I asked her, hearing raised voices.

She dashed past me without comment.

I veered over to the library door. Nate followed curiously, as did my mother.

It took a moment to fully register what I was seeing.

Winston Van Brewer and Trawley Wellington were on either side of Bibi, whose hands were pressed on their chests as they leaned toward each other, arguing over her head. They were both red-faced, flinging insults and snarling.

"Stop it!" I said, hurling myself between them and holding out my arms. "Step back!"

Winston stood his ground, but Chancellor Wellington looked down at his feet as if surprised to see where they were positioned and did as I asked, clasping his hands behind his back.

"Winston," Bibi said, "please give me some space."

He moved the tiniest bit backwards but stuck out his chin and addressed the chancellor. "This isn't over. You have no right barging in on this deal."

"I have money," Trawley said smoothly, "and I have interest. Therefore, I have every right."

"But Callahan House belongs to Callahan College! It has always been that way, and it should always *be* that way."

"It's *never* been that way," Ilse said as she entered the library with Penelope and Brody trailing behind her.

She moved next to her sister and stared down the college president. "The Callahan family has always maintained possession of this property. It may have *felt* like the college owned it because the Callahans were generous enough to let you use it from time to time, but let's keep the facts straight here."

"Thank you, Ilse," Bibi said.

"You know what I mean," Winston entreated his hostess directly.

"I do," she said. "We've had an unspoken agreement with the college. And if it were up to me, I probably would sell you Callahan House today—"

"Don't be hasty. I'll give you more money than he will," the chancellor interjected. "*Far* more. I'll make you an offer you can't refuse."

That didn't seem like the right quote. Or did the chancellor fancy himself the Godfather of Stonedale? If so, I didn't want to think about that for one instant longer, especially since I'd just refused. Well, refused to do his bidding, anyway.

"Let's remember that I, as a member of the Callahan family, also have a vote in what happens to the estate." Ilse's lips turned up. "And I am not convinced that a sale is in the family's best interests."

Both men turned toward her. Their expressions conveyed their frustration but neither said a word.

"We'll be in touch," she said firmly. "And that, gentlemen, is that."

"I don't think so," Margot said, stepping forward, her eyes glittering. "That is *not* that, because Bibi already promised to sell this to Winston. You did, Bibi."

Bibi nodded. "I said I'd *consider* it, but there was no agreement made to sell it to you. No terms have been discussed. No paperwork has been signed. And to be fair, that was before Ilse arrived, which has changed everything."

Winston put his arm around his wife. "Thank you, Margot. I've been saying the same thing. I viewed our conversation as a verbal contract, Bibi. The appearance of Elsa doesn't make one whit of difference—"

"Ilse," Margot said, mechanically.

"Thank you, as always, my love." Winston smiled at her. She lifted her shoulders in a charming acknowledgment.

Bibi had begun to reply when Detective Ortiz strolled into the library. He caught my eye and dipped his chin.

Fresh energy surged through me.

I clapped my hands, then smiled into the startled faces around the room. "Excuse me, but could everyone please take a seat? I have something that you all need to hear."

Chapter 22

Everyone was sitting down except Detective Ortiz and Chancellor Wellington—the latter's lean against the wall coupled with a first-rate glower sent the message that he wasn't about to let a mere assistant professor tell him what to do.

So be it.

"Thank you for welcoming me to Larkston. I've really enjoyed getting to know you this fall," I said. "Most of you know that Bibi asked me to see if I could help sort out what happened to Gillian, and I thought you might be interested in an update."

There was an air of anticipation in the room, but no one spoke.

"First, you'll be glad to hear that *The Secrets of Everwell*, the manuscript Bibi wrote about your last summer before college, has been returned to her." I did a scan of faces, but everyone looked equally surprised. "From the beginning, the fact that the manuscript disappeared the same night Gillian was murdered signaled an important connection, but it was difficult to establish what that link might be. "We"—I gestured to Bibi—"thought it might have to do with the revelation of secrets."

"Our high school drama," Bibi added. "Things better left in the past."

The group members caught each other's eyes. From what I could gauge by their expressions, the thought prompted a blend of embarrassment and nostalgia.

"We believe that Gillian had the manuscript in her possession when she was killed and that the murderer took it. Which made it all the more surprising when the manuscript showed up again, having been mailed to the police." There were some exclamations and muted comments. "After Bibi had been provided with a copy, I took the opportunity to read through it completely, and although there were indeed some aspects of intrigue and emotion, there wasn't anything that pointed to anyone directly."

Bibi raised her hand. "Let me apologize again, everyone, for writing about our lives. I never imagined that it would be seen by anyone other than myself."

"Bygones," Winston said, as he adjusted a cuff link.

"Why are you telling us all of this?" Penelope seemed especially intrigued.

I smiled at her. "I'm getting to that. The manuscript may have captured some of the actual drama from that summer in detail, but the one glaring difference between real life and the manuscript involves the ending of the story. The book suggests that Hudson Shane killed Ilse. We now know that is untrue."

"Obviously." Ilse raised her glass. "Because here I am."

There was laughter around the room.

I waited for it to die down before continuing. "When the manuscript showed up at the police department, it didn't make any sense. The working theory had been that there was a struggle over the manuscript itself. Presumably the murderer realized from the title—or from something Gillian told them about it—that there could be damaging information within. In other words, the murderer took it to protect themselves."

"Then why would they bother mailing it back?" Margot asked. "Fairly absurd, isn't it?

"Because once they'd read it, they realized that the manuscript pointed a guilty finger at Hudson, rather than at themselves, for

Ilse's murder. It actually would steer attention *away* from them."

There were widespread sounds of surprise.

"In addition, it served yet another purpose, aiming suspicion toward Bibi."

"How so?" Penelope tucked her hair behind her ears, as if preparing herself to better hear the evidence.

"Since it has been suggested that Hudson and Jamie were run off the road." Around the room, faces clouded at the memory. I hated having to drag them through the tragedy another time. "I'm very sorry about what has happened to all of your friends."

Brody cleared his throat. "But how is the car accident related to Bibi?"

"She accused Hudson of killing her sister...in print. The manuscript gives her motive because it shows that she thought he was guilty."

Winston grimaced. "But Jamie was in the car too."

"The spouse is always the first to be looked at by the police," Margot said, "and it might have been a mistake, anyway, going after Hudson's car without knowing Jamie was inside."

Bibi made a small sound, like a stifled moan.

Margot turned to her. "Oh, I'm sorry, Bibi. We know you would *never* do anything like that."

"Margot is just drawing on information from her crime-show habit right now," Winston said apologetically.

"He's right. I don't know what I'm talking about," Margot said. "Please, dearest friend, forgive me."

"We all know how much you loved Jamie," Penelope chimed in. "That has never been in doubt, not once, by any of us, over the years."

Bibi sniffled but fluttered her hand at me to continue.

I picked up where I'd left off. "The murderer might have thought that the manuscript could shine a light onto Gillian's murder as well...suggesting that if Bibi killed Hudson as revenge for Ilse's death, she might be willing to go after his wife too."

"Ten years later?" Brody asked. "Makes no sense."

"Perhaps she was just waiting for the perfect moment," Margot mused. "Statistically speaking, it's surprising how long someone might—"

"You're doing it again," Winston interrupted her. "This is not a television show. You need to stop."

"Sorry, sorry," she said, waving one hand as if to erase what she'd just said.

"You don't believe I would do that, do you?" Bibi asked me.

"No," I reassured her. "But I have to walk us through the thought process."

"Wait," Ilse said slowly, "you're saying someone killed Gillian to get the manuscript, but once they realized that the manuscript made another person look guilty, they sent it to the police in order to turn the attention onto that person?"

"Yes. That's been established," Penelope said impatiently. "The big question is: who would do that?"

"There's another big question that we need to address first." I turned to Ilse. "Who *are* you?"

She paled but mustered up a confused expression. "What are you talking about? I'm Ilse Callahan."

"Prove it."

She exposed the dove tattoo on her wrist.

Bibi pointed to it. "Yes. That's proof."

"Not really. Anyone can get a tattoo, Bibi, at any time."

"That's true, Lila," my mother chimed in. "There's a *flourishing* industry in New York. Around the country as well, but I can only speak about local ink. You'd be amazed at the quality of the artwork..." She trailed off when she realized that everyone was staring at her. "Just trying to contribute. Never mind."

I turned back to Ilse. “Jensen Callahan never married you.”

“He absolutely did.” Ilse sputtered and looked around the room as if to find agreement with her sentiment.

None was forthcoming.

“If so, the timeline doesn’t work. You said you ran away with Jensen that night, but Ilse was at Everwell. We saw her in a picture.”

“Lila found it in the study,” Bibi told the rest of the room.

Something moved behind Ilse’s eyes. “I went to the lake first, before running away.”

“To do what?”

“To watch everyone.” She shrugged. “I did that sometimes.”

“She did,” Bibi concurred.

“Okay, onto more incriminating evidence, then. I found your ID cards, the ones with the name Alycia Greenwich on them.”

Ilse laughed. “That’s my cover name. Jensen and I both took on false identities in order to disappear. We were Mr. and Mrs. Greenwich. We didn’t want anyone to find us. And guess what, they didn’t.” She leaned back and crossed her arms.

“That’s a lie. I don’t know where Jensen is now or what name he’s using, but he’s not online anywhere under that name.”

Ilse opened her mouth to speak.

“And you *cannot* be Ilse Callahan. She died that night at the lake.”

She clamped her lips shut.

There were gasps all around the room, Bibi’s being the loudest of all. “Lila, what are you talking about? They dragged the lake multiple times, and she wasn’t there. They couldn’t find her. They never found her.”

I looked at the detective, who again dipped his chin.

“She wasn’t in the lake. She was submerged instead in the flooded quarry.”

Bibi stared at me. "What in the world makes you think that?"

"That's where the evidence pointed," I said briskly. I didn't want to go any further into the explanation, which was that seeing Brody's statue and my mother's dress one right after the other had focused my attention on stones and sparked the quarry theory, which I'd called in to Detective Ortiz. Honestly, I was as surprised as anyone that he'd confirmed it, but here we were.

"We do have ample proof," the detective said. "The family provided it."

"Wait, wait, wait. What? Ilse is dead again?" Penelope burst into tears and put her hands over her face. Brody patted her back.

"She always was," Margot said softly.

"No, I'm...I'm right here," the woman formerly known as Ilse protested, half-heartedly. "There must be some mistake. You can all see me, right? Whoever you found is someone else."

"If you subscribe to that theory, perhaps you'd like to take a DNA test to prove that you and Bibi are sisters? The officers can swab your cheek right now." I waved in the detective's direction.

"Definitely. Sure. I mean..." She looked wildly around the room, then her shoulders sagged. "All *right*. I'm not Ilse. Whatever."

"I knew it!" Nate said triumphantly from the corner.

"What is your name?" Bibi asked through gritted teeth.

"Alycia Greenwich." She curtsied. "At your service."

"Why did you come here?" Winston demanded.

She did a little shimmy in his direction, taunting him. "That's for me to know and you to find out."

This was getting weird.

"Oh, it feels so good not to have to be whatshername anymore." Alycia clapped her hands and sneered. "She was so *boring*. Always knitting and talking softly. And smiling—so much smiling."

It was as though an entirely different person had shown up. No telling what she might do.

Alycia began humming loudly.

Keeping an eye on her, I addressed the group. "She came for Callahan House, at least a part, possibly the whole—"

"I see where you're going with that," Bibi said. "I could have been the next victim, if she decided to try and get the entire inheritance."

"Callahan House is my dream," Alycia sang as she swayed back and forth, "and I am its one and only queen."

Winston harrumphed, probably thinking of his own desire for Callahan House.

"Wow," said Bibi, eyeing Alycia's performance.

She stopped singing abruptly and gave Bibi a dirty look. "So what if I did try to get something for my family?"

"You're not a Callahan," Bibi said.

"But I *am* Darien and Alice's niece. They deserve a taste of the good life too. They've lived here longer than *you* have, squatter."

Bibi crossed her arms. "That's how you knew about the tattoo, isn't it? My mother asked the Callahans if she should mention it to the police. Alice could have overheard them."

"Aren't you a smart cookie!" She stuck out her tongue. "Yes, she did, though I also saw a picture of it somewhere years ago. But you can safely assume that they overheard everything that was going on at Callahan House and they told me about it in detail. Always have. We're very close—I was named after my aunt, obviously, and I even came to visit when I was little. So many times. Not that any of you noticed. You were all so wrapped up in *yourselves*." Alycia made a face. "Anyway, I made a plan right after they said you were selling the place and they were afraid about what would happen. It's not like they had any retirement program."

"But I would have made sure they were well taken care of,"

Bibi said.

"Says you. There's nothing in writing."

"There doesn't have to be. I care about them. And if they were worried, why didn't they talk to me?"

"Why do you think?" Alycia snarled. "They hate you."

"They *hate* me?"

"Of course. They lived in that tiny shack for decades, watching you worm your way from the other shack into the main house...using your body to inflame Jamie Callahan's lust. Then later, when you had used him all up, you killed him."

Bibi gasped. "I didn't use anything! We fell in love. And I didn't kill him—that's outrageous."

"Thou shalt be judged and judged harshly." She stood up, put both arms out in front of her, and began humming again.

"Hold on there, Alycia," I said. "We're not done yet. Have a seat."

She tried to ignore me, but I summoned my best version of that which is used in classrooms around the globe during situations like this: the stone-cold teacher stare.

Alycia plunked back down, pouting. Either she had wanted to finish her bizarre conjuring act, or the fact that her jig was up was starting to sink in.

I looked around the room. "To solve Gillian's murder, we need to solve Ilse's. The manuscript connection strongly suggests that the second was performed to cover up the first...or, at least to keep the truth of the first one buried. For this part, we need to focus in on the secrets that everyone was trying so desperately to keep the summer of Everwell."

Some people began to shift in their seats uncomfortably.

Chapter 23

"The information I've gathered is primarily from the manuscript, which we know Bibi fictionalized, and from conversations with all of you. I don't want to offend anyone, but we need to dive in. As we go along, please correct me if I'm wrong about something."

"You don't have to be so careful," Margot scoffed. "That was years ago. We've all moved on, Lila."

"I'm glad to hear you say that, because the primary issue appears to be your affair with Hudson."

She smirked. "By affair, you mean stolen kisses. We never did more than that. It was kid stuff."

"But remember you made me buy that pregnancy test?" Penelope spoke up. "Was that for Hudson? I thought it was for Winston."

Margot scowled at her.

Penelope winced. "I'm sorry, I don't know what I'm saying. Ignore me, everyone. I'm extremely upset."

I pushed forward. "In any case, Margot, you *did* meet up with Hudson more than once, which was what you told the Larks."

"Maybe." She smoothed the skin near her temple. "Who can remember?"

"We all do," Winston said sullenly.

"But you've forgiven me, my love," Margot said, in an encouraging voice. She put her hand on his arm. "Right?"

"Right. It was so long ago." He took a drink from his highball glass.

"How can that possibly be worth mentioning at this point?" Margot turned to me. "I don't understand why we're discussing it."

"Because Penelope believed Brody was cheating on her, and Brody was angry with Penelope for thinking that. It caused problems in their relationship, which they confided to Gillian."

"And Gillian told Hudson," Penelope added. "That's important too."

"Well, Hudson already knew," Margot said, with one of her signature eye rolls. "I mean, he was there *with* me, wasn't he?"

Winston made a sound almost like a whimper.

"Sorry, my love," she said to him.

"But things changed once Hudson knew that Brody and I were fighting," Penelope explained angrily. "He goaded us on, especially when he had been drinking. On some nights, he'd taunt Brody about not being 'man enough' to keep me, and on other nights, he'd pull Brody aside and tell him to dump me because I was being a shrew. Hudson was one of those people who enjoyed making others uncomfortable."

"Hudson *did* like to stir things up," Margot said dreamily. She must have felt the widespread glares this interpretation evoked, as she apologized a moment later.

Bibi cleared her throat. "Jamie talked to Hudson about it, told him to cut it out. But Hudson didn't want anyone—not even his best friends—telling him what to do. As soon as he heard a rumor about Ilse making a play for Jamie by climbing into his bed, he amplified it. It spread around school like wildfire."

"That's a lie!" Alycia screamed. "I would never have debased myself like that."

"You aren't even Ilse! You just admitted that to us," Margot reminded her.

Alycia crossed her arms and resumed her moping.

"I don't think it was true, either," Bibi said. "Hudson might even have started it."

"The fallout from that summer had far-reaching consequences." I went on. "The friendship between Jamie and Hudson was never the same, was it, Bibi?"

"No," she said quietly.

"And Winston, you and Hudson were never the same either, were you?"

"Bygones," he said, sniffing haughtily. "We let go of that childishness almost immediately."

"That's not what I meant. I'm talking about something else."

He affected a pained look. "I don't know to what you are referring."

Winston clearly wasn't going to volunteer anything. Time to get more specific. "I wondered if you, from the night of the bonfire forward, felt indebted to him?"

"What do you mean?"

"For covering up the fact that you put Ilse's body in the lake at the abandoned quarry?"

Winston's jaw dropped. Gasps echoed around the room.

"Win, you took Ilse to the quarry?" Margot stared at him as if she'd never seen him before.

"I'm confused," my mother complained. "What is happening right now?"

"The one Ilse made a play for was *Win*," I said. "And Margot knew it."

"So you're trying to get someone to confess?" My mother stage-whispered loudly enough for the whole room to hear.

I didn't answer, watching Margot and Winston.

"You did that, Win?" Margot asked him, incredulously.

I held my breath. Bring it, Margot.

She put a hand on his face. "That's the nicest thing anyone has ever done for me."

Win kissed her.

Not at all the confrontation I'd been hoping for.

"Wait a minute, Margot killed Ilse?" My mother whispered again, as if she was watching one of her beloved noir films. All she was missing was a box of popcorn.

I put up a finger in the hold-on-one-minute sign, but Penelope went right ahead and shushed her.

"Is this true?" Bibi addressed both of them. "You killed my sister?"

"I *didn't* kill her." Winston said.

"But Lila just said—"

He adjusted his tie. "To be precise, I found her body on the rocks by the shore." The calmness he was displaying was unsettling.

"Why did you move her, then?" I asked.

"I was trying to help."

"How?"

Winston and Margot locked eyes, seemingly having an entire conversation.

"Go on," he said.

Margot looked around the group. "Yes, it was my boyfriend Ilse had gone after. It had happened earlier, but I also saw her lurking in the trees that night. She was there when Hudson and I...you know...slipped off. Afterwards, she hissed something at me from the leaves. I didn't engage her, but I guess she figured that since Hudson and I had hooked up, Win was fair game. When the other Larks went home, I doubled back and went looking for her. I was right, she was waiting on one of the cliffs about halfway to the bridge. We exchanged words and she started moving around, waving her arms. I guess she lost her footing, because one minute she was there, and the next minute she wasn't. But I didn't know what happened after that. I looked down and couldn't see anything."

Winston said, "All I knew was that I heard Margot's voice, and I was worried she might be accused of something disreputable. It would have been lurid."

"We were king and queen of the prom," Margot added primly, as if that explained everything.

Brody made a sound of disgust.

"She was already dead," Winston said flatly. "I didn't kill her."

"I didn't know, until right now, what you'd done," Margot said to Winston. "I didn't know you moved her body."

"You didn't need to know."

"Wait, you two have never discussed it?" I asked. "That's hard to believe."

Margot shook her head.

Winston backed her up.

"When Ilse showed up here at Callahan House," Margot said, "I can't even begin to describe how relieved I was to see her alive and well. I'd always felt somewhat guilty about not going down to the shore to check on her."

"*Somewhat*? You should have done so," Penelope said.

"In my own defense, it was very dark, not to mention dangerous to climb down the cliffs alone. I was extremely upset. Yes, I was angry, but I was also a bit scared of her, if you must know. She was aggressive. It was a confusing time."

"But you could have *told* us," Bibi said bitterly. "You saw the pain we were going through, not knowing where she was."

"I don't know, Bibi. Technically, Ilse *could* have gotten up and run away," Winston said. "Who's to say that she didn't?"

"*You're* the one who moved her body," I reminded him.

"Oh, right," he said.

Wow.

"When did you do that?" Brody asked. "You and Hudson met Jamie and me by the dock."

"I pulled over near the bridge on the way home, went back for Ilse, and took her to Shane Quarry."

The room fell quiet.

I launched back into the story. "Then Hudson's family found her body not long afterwards, right? And covered it up. They knew it would be a scandal."

"For *them*," Winston said peevishly. "It would have looked bad for them. They didn't do it for me."

"Were you trying to frame Hudson by putting her there?" I asked.

He shrugged. "Doesn't matter."

"It does, but let's move on and say that in any case, they did cover it up. It benefitted you. Why, years later, did you repay that favor by running Hudson and Jamie off the road?"

"I am extending yet another most emphatic denial."

"Are you sure? Because you and Hudson were both up for the college president job at the same time, as you told me in your office, so it would have helped you in more ways than one."

He took a long pull on his drink. "I am sure."

"Also he was blackmailing you about Ilse," I added, on a hunch.

"How did you know about that?" Margot blinked rapidly. "I didn't even know what exactly Hudson was holding over his head, but I did know about the money Win kept shelling out to him."

"Be quiet, Margot." Winston said calmly.

"And you *did* kill Gillian." I locked eyes with him.

"Why would you say that?"

"Because a little while ago, you referred to Ilse as 'Elsa.'"

"So?" His tone suggested he was humoring me.

"That's the name Bibi used for Ilse in the manuscript, which means *you* must have read it."

He scoffed. "The entire police department had access to that."

"Because you sent it to them. After you stole it when you killed Gillian."

He denied it with a quick shake of his head, but it was clear that his thoughts were scrambling.

"Do you want me to go on?" I asked. "Shall we talk about Tacey too?"

"Win, is it true?" Margot stood up and confronted her husband.

He opened his mouth, but no words came out.

She stomped her foot. "Tell me!"

That seemed to startle him into speech. "You killed for me; I killed for you, my love."

Margot's face went white. "But I *didn't* kill for you. Ilse fell."

He considered this, took another long drink from his glass, and set it down on the table next to him. "Tell yourself whatever you want. I heard you scream 'he's mine,' right before her body came hurtling down the incline."

"That's a lie," she whispered. "And you killed Gillian."

"Gillian showed me Bibi's book. She was very excited and wanted to publish it. I thought the whole tawdry affair might be spelled out in there, and I couldn't let that happen. I happen to enjoy our life as it is and wanted to keep it that way. Margot, I did it *for you.*"

"How could you?" Margot's hand flew up to her throat.

"What about Tacey?" I asked him.

"She was talking too much," he said, sounding annoyed. "Couldn't have that. Though her tip line did come in handy both before and after her death."

"You were trying to shape the story through the whole manuscript issue. Cherry picking details that would make others seem guilty."

"The Throckhams did not have impeccable timing, Lila. They needed a nudge more often than not."

He stood up and smoothed his tie, then went over to the window, where he surveyed the view. "I'm sorry, Bibi, about this messy business. I hope we can put it behind us."

She didn't respond.

"And I'm sorry about this magnificent house, though I think I did you a favor by clearing away some space. That cottage was so ratty."

"You set the fire?" She spoke through clenched teeth. "You could have killed us all."

"I thought it might make you want to leave. Or at least stop asking so many damn questions. And you have to admit, a new boathouse for the crew team would be terrific there."

He laughed.

"Or maybe some stables? We could add a polo field..."

As he prattled on, I nodded at the detective in the doorway, who gave me a grudging look of respect before stepping forward.

Several officers followed him.

My mother swooped in and patted me on the back. "Well done, darling," she said proudly. "That was *very* exciting."

Chapter 24

My mother and I were sitting in the parlor with Bibi, who had invited us back to Callahan House to spend Christmas Eve with her. We had enjoyed a delicious meal and delightful conversation, and I'd given Bibi the stained glass panel, which she said she would cherish. A piano concerto was playing in the background, the fire was warm, and for the first time in a long time, I felt relaxed.

Bibi took a sip of tea. "Thank you for keeping me company. I needed a break from the whole...crowd."

"Our pleasure." I smiled at our host. "If you're free tomorrow, we'd love to have you for a visit in Stonedale."

"I'll think about it, but I may sleep through Christmas altogether. I'm exhausted." She set down her tea and picked up a cluster of yarn from her knitting bag, which she began winding into a ball.

I could imagine how tired she was, given what the past week had wrought. "Where are the Larks?" I had expected that they'd be here tonight.

"From what I hear, the Van Brewers are spending the holidays lawyering up. I don't think we'll be seeing much of each other anymore. I had no idea that they were such terrible people."

"Do you mean Winston?" my mother asked.

"I mean both of them. He's obviously a monster, and, well, Margot is far less compassionate than I'd have guessed," Bibi said.

"That's putting it kindly," Violet exclaimed. "She left your sister *lying* there all alone! It's unforgivable."

"Let's just say that I'm more than ready to allow a little distance to come between us."

"What about the Isabella Dare Papers that she's organizing for Callahan College?" I wondered.

"I'll hold up my end of the bargain, but it will be for the college's sake, not hers."

"How about the professors?" Violet asked. "They're such a nice couple. I'm glad that they didn't do anything disgraceful."

"Pen and Brody flew to Florida for winter break—they want to recuperate from the stress of the semester on the beach. He claimed to be seeking artistic inspiration in the ocean, which may be code for an excessive amount of scuba diving, who knows."

"And how are you doing?" I looked at Bibi. "Honestly."

"I am relieved to finally have answers, even though realizing that one of my lifelong friends killed four people, including my husband, and covered up the death of my sister was a lot to take in. Shocking, to be honest. I'm still processing everything. But I can't tell you how much it means to me to know what really happened...with Gillian, with Ilse, with everything. Thank you, Lila."

"Happy to have been able to help."

"Can you imagine if Lila hadn't discovered the Ilse situation? You'd be stuck in this house and half of your money would have been gone like *that*." My mother snapped her fingers.

"I wouldn't have minded about the money," Bibi said. "But I am ready to leave Callahan House."

A door slammed upstairs.

"And *that* too," Bibi said.

"Who's up there?" Violet eyed the ceiling apprehensively. "I thought we were alone."

I remembered Bibi mentioning that she thought the Callahans communicated with her sometimes and wondered if she'd tell my mother the same thing.

"I don't think anyone is ever truly alone here," Bibi said vaguely.

Violet saw right through it. "You have ghosts? Your asking price just skyrocketed! That is a *premium* asset."

Bibi laughed.

"Have you chosen a buyer?" I asked her.

She smiled. "Obviously, it's not going to be Winston."

"Excellent decision," Violet said. "He doesn't deserve a thing."

"How about Chancellor Wellington?" Not that I wanted her to sell to him, after the way he had behaved. He was just the logical next guess.

"I won't be selling to him, either." She finished winding the yarn and put it into the bag at her feet.

"He claimed that he would give you a great deal of money for it. You'd be set for life," Violet said.

"I didn't care for his pressure tactics and I told him so to his face." Bibi winked at me, knowing I would enjoy imagining that. "I've thought long and hard about this. Despite the fact that Winston was the one pushing the idea originally, I do believe the students and faculty at the college will have a use for Callahan House, and I trust them to preserve the history of the site. They'll have a new president soon, so it wouldn't be as though I'm doing anything for Winston's career. He's out no matter what."

"Good riddance," Violet murmured.

"What happens next?"

"I've reached out to the board of trustees. They were elated and said to expect their offer very soon. We'll see what they come up with. I'm sure it will be more than fair."

"Don't forget to mention the ghosts," Violet urged her.

"What about the tours you have here?" I asked.

"It will be up to the college whether they want to continue them. I did suggest that it might work well as a museum, if they were so inclined. But they may turn the space into offices or classrooms."

"Anyone would be lucky to spend time here," I said, glancing appreciatively around the parlor. "I certainly have. Thank you again for all of your hospitality."

"It's been my pleasure." Bibi said. "And don't think you're getting away from me so easily. We're going to meet for *many* lunches in the future. I still want to read your manuscripts too."

"I'd love that."

"Will you please email them to me tonight when you get home? I won't take no for an answer this time."

"I will. Where are you moving?"

"I have my eye on a little house next to the park at the center of town. It is newly remodeled, much smaller, and has everything I need, including a study. Plus, I'll be able to walk everywhere from there. The owner is a friend of mine, and she has agreed to sell it to me as soon as I can close on Callahan House. I'm hoping to have everything done within a month or so. Oh!" She looked stricken. "I'm sorry about all that work you put into organizing my study here."

I laughed. "Now it will be easy for the movers to transport the file cabinets to the new place."

"True. But I suppose I'll have to give away most of my books. I can't even imagine tackling that project." She sighed. "In fact, take what you want tonight on your way out."

"I know," my mother said, waving her hands around energetically. "Host a *huge* party and give away all the books in goodie bags! You'll be the talk of the town!"

"I should have done that last week," Bibi said ruefully.

"Or you could leave the books here for the students," I said. "It's an extraordinary collection. Maybe they would put up a plaque with your name on it. Think of it: the Bibi Callahan Mystery Library."

"What a wonderful idea." She paused. "The library part, I mean. Not the other part. No one needs my name hanging on their wall."

"I was thinking a large door sign," I said. "Engraved."

Bibi ignored that. "Anyway, now that we have *that* settled, I could use your help with another challenge...what to do about the Flemms."

My mother shivered. "Ugh. Those horrid people tried to scam you! And fake Ilse told you that they hated you."

"I know, Violet, but I do feel responsible for their future. Despite how they went about it—"

"Trying to perpetuate fraud!" My mother cut in.

"Alycia was the one who did that," I said. "And now she'll do some time for it."

"I understand their concerns," Bibi said. "This *has* been their home too, and they don't have any retirement fund. Would it be strange to give them some of the proceeds of the Callahan House sale?"

"*I* think so," Violet said. "Wait, are they still here on the property right now?"

"Yes."

"That won't do. You can't be *alone* with them."

"I'm not afraid of Alice and Darien," Bibi told her. "They may not care much for me as a person, but they're not dangerous."

"Famous last words," Violet muttered. "Look at their niece."

I had an idea. "You should tell them you're thinking of sharing the proceeds. Then even if they are harboring ill will toward you, they'll be less likely to harm you because they'll want their payday.

Not to be crass or anything."

Bibi nodded. "You could be right."

"Do you want us to go over to the cottage with you?" I offered. "I'd be glad to accompany you."

"Actually, yes. Why don't we bring them some cookies too? I have tons left from the party, far more than I could ever eat." Bibi stood and picked up her tea.

"Nothing goes better with money than cookies," Violet replied.

"Cookies go with everything. They're one of the most persuasive foods." I followed them into the kitchen, where Bibi piled a plate high.

After she added clear wrap, we put on our coats and walked out the back door. I went first, sweeping my cell phone flashlight back and forth along the snowy path for visibility. When we came around the last bend, I stopped short to avoid banging into Alice, who stood there with her own plate of cookies.

She let out a little squeak.

"It's just us," Bibi said, passing me. "Bringing you cookies."

Alice held up her own plate, also full of cookies.

Who was trying to persuade whom here?

Darien stepped out from behind her—I hadn't even seen him in the shadows. "We were coming to apologize, Bibi. We're sorry about all the hoopla. Alycia's a good girl with a big heart—"

I would *not* have described her that way.

"—but she shouldn't have done what she did. She's got problems—has ever since she was younger. But we didn't see much of her, as she lived out there in California. My sister always took the best care of her that she could, but she's gone now, and Alycia has been on her own. We thought everything was fine, but obviously now we know better. We didn't know what she was up to, passing herself off as Ilse, until we saw her in action at the night of the party. She told us you'd offered her a room at the house so as not to inconvenience us and we believed her. We know how generous you are."

"Oh!" Bibi said, clearly surprised.

"But I heard you talking in the great room..." I addressed Darien.

Everyone turned to look at me.

"Something about getting it done? Working her magic?"

After a moment, Darien nodded. "Alycia said she was going to ask Bibi on our behalf if we could take over more of the tour work. Alice and I have been auditing local history classes over at the college, and we think we could add a little something special to the tours. Bibi has let us live here for so long—"

"For *free*," Alice said. "So kind."

"—and we wanted to give something back."

I think it's safe to say that the three of us were completely stunned by what we heard.

"Why don't we all go up to the house," Bibi suggested. "I have an idea I'd like to run by you as well."

Chapter 25

The next day, I was back in Stonedale; my bungalow felt especially small after spending so much time in Bibi's mansion, but it was definitely cozy. My mother and I had just finished exchanging gifts when the doorbell rang. When I pulled open the door, I was surprised to see Bibi holding a bag and plate of cookies like the ones she'd given Alice and Darien. She handed the plate to me. "Happy Christmas!"

I returned the greeting, took her coat, then offered her a seat.

"We're gathered around the coffee table tree," I said. "Not a widely known practice, but as you can see, we don't have a lot of space." She admired the red ribbons and silver bells I'd looped around a miniature pine tree in a pot that I was planning to plant in the backyard after the holidays. Then she took in the rest of the place, which was achievable with one swift turn of the head.

"This is lovely, Lila. Reminds me of my cottage."

Our eyes met, as we silently honored her lost home.

"So glad you stopped by," I said. "How has your day been?"

I returned to the sofa where my mother was waiting and patted the cushion. Bibi sat down between us.

"Well," she said, "it's been a whirlwind. I invited Alice and Darien for brunch, and we had a thorough conversation about tours. They're going to lead the rest of them during December, which is perfect because our regular guide took a job at the college doing student orientation events. Then when the college takes over, the Flemms will pitch their services as tour guides, and we'll try to work out a deal."

"So you heard from the board of trustees?" Violet inquired.

"Right after the Flemms left, my phone rang and the trustees made me a very generous offer indeed. They also agreed with my proposal to let Alice and Darien live in the guest cottage as long as they'd like, so they won't have to move. The board waived the inspection, as they want the house no matter what, and we'll close on the deal very soon."

"Congratulations!"

"I can't wait to move into my new place. You'll both be invited to my housewarming party."

Violet went into the kitchen. I had no idea what she was doing in there, rummaging around, until she returned with three flutes of champagne. I didn't know there was champagne in the house. She must have gone shopping when I wasn't looking.

"Cheers for wonderful things," she said. We all toasted and took a sip.

Bibi withdrew two packages from her bag. She handed a long slender one to my mother and a thick square one to me. My mother unwrapped hers first, which was a hand-painted scarf with dragonflies.

"Don't be too excited," Bibi said. "I made it myself."

"Then it's a one-of-a-kind art piece." Violet put it on and threw the long end over her shoulder. "I absolutely *love* it. Thank you."

Bibi urged me to open mine next.

I unpeeled the paper to discover a hand-painted scarf with butterflies draped around something hard.

"Did you make this too? How beautiful."

"Yes, sorry." She laughed. "And the butterfly is symbolic. It's been a delight to see you blossoming in your writing and career."

I was so moved I couldn't even speak.

"And keep unwrapping...there's more."

I carefully unwound the scarf to discover what looked like a manuscript bound within a blank cardboard cover. She watched me closely as I opened it to read the title page: *The Study of Secrets.*

"Did you revise the Everwell manuscript?"

"No. That one's going into the vault forever. I may even burn it—"

"Please don't. Save it for posterity as the first-ever Athena Bolt development in the Isabella Dare papers."

"I'll consider that. But this," she pointed at the book in my hand, "is the one I've been finishing this fall."

"Is it..." I was so hopeful I almost couldn't breathe.

Bibi read my face. "Yes. It's another Athena Bolt book."

"The first one in decades," I said.

"Took me long enough."

"Has anyone else read this?"

"You'll be the first. I'd also like you to write a foreword, if you would, as the world's leading Isabella Dare scholar."

I gasped. "I'd be honored. Though I am *not* the world's leading Isabella Dare scholar."

"Wait a second. Those competitors from the conference never wrote anything, did they?" Bibi watched me closely.

"No."

"And have you come across anyone else writing on the series?"

"No."

She broke into a wide smile. "So right now, you're the *only* Isabella Dare scholar. See? My description holds true. And you deserve it. You've already dedicated so much time and energy to my books."

"It's been my pleasure, a hundred percent."

"Also, I've decided that there's no sense in hiding the fact that Bibi Callahan is Isabella Dare anymore. That will make things easier for your critical study, won't it? You'll be able to cite our interviews directly, at the very least. I know there are other benefits too."

I wiped away a tear. "I don't know what I did to deserve you, Bibi. You're like my fairy godmother."

"Thank *you*. You supported my books, and you've been a true friend." She brushed a tear away too. "Truth be told, you're like the daughter I never had."

"What can I do to join in on the celebration?" Violet scooted down the sofa toward us. "Maybe I could contribute some art for the book?"

Bibi looked thoughtful. "Would you be interested in doing some cover or marketing art? If we can find a publisher who is interested in the book, maybe we could write that into the contract negotiations."

"What a great idea," Violet murmured.

"It's not the usual thing, but then again, neither am I."

"None of us are, darling. Here's to unusual women." Violet raised her glass to clink ours.

"When do you go back to New York?" Bibi asked, after we'd all taken a drink.

"About that..." My mother set down her glass and turned to me. "What would you think about me staying in Stonedale for a while? I need a change from the city. The art-in disaster confirmed it. And I *desperately* want to be closer to you and Calista. What do you say?"

"I would love it! Calista would too. Especially now that there's a wedding to plan."

"We'll have so much fun. And don't worry about me cramping your style. I wouldn't stay here," she said, casting a doubtful glance around my tiny bungalow. "No offense, darling. It's...adorable. I just need more *space* to do my art. You understand."

"Of course."

"Then it's settled," she said, clasping her hands together. "Maybe I can take some of your classes! Wouldn't that be a hoot?"

Did my mother say she wanted to *take my classes*? The idea clattered around my mind like an accelerating train.

She bounded happily ahead with her ideas. I had a familiar sensation of racing after her, trying to keep up.

"And now that I know you're on board, darling, I have more good news—I've already signed a lease! It's the most *fabulous* little house around the corner, almost exactly halfway between you and Calista."

Bibi looked back and forth between us, smiling.

The doorbell rang, giving me a much-needed moment to process all of my mother's announcements.

Nate stood there, holding a wreath with a red bow.

"Merry Christmas!" I stepped outside and pulled the door closed behind me to keep the heat in. The snow was falling gently and the world seemed hushed.

"I figured you didn't have one since you've been away." He handed me the wreath, which I hung on the nail sticking out of the door. We stood for a moment admiring it, and I thanked him.

"Bibi and my mom are here. Will you come inside for a drink before you go? We're having champagne."

Nate seemed to waver slightly.

I peered closely at him. "Or have you already had a bucket of Christmas cheer?"

"Not a drop." He fixed his eyes on mine—the blue was even more vivid than usual against the white landscape.

"You seem a tad indecisive, my friend."

"That's because I'm trying to decide how to tell you something."

I shivered. "What's wrong?"

Nate waved that away. "Nothing."

"Oh, do you have some additional sidekick intel?"

"In a manner of speaking." He rubbed his hands together. "Here goes. You're one of my best friends, and you know how I feel about you."

"Yes."

His eyes widened. "You *know* that I'm in love with you?"

"No. I meant that I know we're best friends." I stared at him. "Wait, *what* did you say?"

"Surprise! I love you." Nate laughed, then took a shaky breath. "That came out weird. Sorry."

Shocked, I didn't respond.

He rubbed his chin. "Is it a surprise? Maybe it's not a surprise. I wish I had asked you out years ago and worked up to this declaration properly, but the timing never seemed right. Calista and Francisco's engagement put things into perspective, though. I do *not* want to wait any longer if you think you could love me too someday."

My heart pounded. We already spent as much time together as possible, told each other everything, and protected one another. We'd laughed, we'd cried, we'd survived department meetings. But we had studiously avoided addressing the undeniable sparks between us. As the memories flashed through my mind, I had the sensation that something was falling into place: I was all in. I just hadn't recognized it. The realization delivered a rush of joy, the likes of which I'd never experienced before.

Nate was still talking. "And if you can't love me in that way, don't worry. I have a backup plan. We'll pretend this never happened, because I refuse to mess up our friendship. Simply consider it an impromptu performance inspired by the viewing of far too many holiday movies. Those can be dangerously poignant, you know. I can't help watching them because they suck you in with their jingle bells and candy canes and happy couples drinking cocoa, but—"

"Stop." I put my hand on his chest. "You're right."

"Seriously?" He covered my hand with his.

"Yes, but *when*—"

"Oh, the day we met. You walked in all quirky and adorable, and I was a goner. That was it for me." He paused. "It took you longer, didn't it? I may be a bit of an acquired taste."

"Maybe, but I know how I feel *now*." I smiled up at him.

He stood there grinning at me, then gave his head a little shake. "We should probably kiss to commemorate this historic moment."

"Please."

I held my breath as he took a step closer and pulled me into his arms. He pressed his lips against mine.

Sweet doesn't even begin to describe it.

He searched my face. "Tell me the truth, Lila. I haven't ruined everything, have I?"

"No," I assured him. "You made everything *right*."

He kissed me again. For a while this time.

When we came up for air, I invited him inside.

"Calista is *never* going to stop saying 'I told you so,'" I murmured, pushing the door open.

"What?"

"Never mind."

As we crossed the threshold, my mother called out merrily, "I forgot to mention that I ran into Nate at the store yesterday. I hope it was okay to invite him to stop by."

"More than okay," I said, looking at Nate.

"Best invite ever," he said, squeezing my hand.

It was a genuine Christmas miracle.

With a little help from my mother.

Photo by Angela Kleinsasser

Cynthia Kuhn

Cynthia Kuhn is an English professor and author of the Lila Maclean Academic Mysteries. Her work has also appeared in *Mystery Most Edible, McSweeney's Quarterly Concern, Copper Nickel, Prick of the Spindle, Mama PhD,* and other publications. Honors for the series include an Agatha Award (best first novel), a William F. Deeck-Malice Domestic Grant, and Lefty Award nominations (best humorous mystery). Originally from upstate New York, she lives in Colorado with her family. For more information, please visit cynthiakuhn.net.

The Lila Maclean Academic Mystery Series
by Cynthia Kuhn

THE SEMESTER OF OUR DISCONTENT (#1)
THE ART OF VANISHING (#2)
THE SPIRIT IN QUESTION (#3)
THE SUBJECT OF MALICE (#4)
THE STUDY OF SECRETS (#5)

Henery Press Mystery Books

And finally, before you go...
Here are a few other mysteries
you might enjoy:

PUMPKINS IN PARADISE

Kathi Daley

A Tj Jensen Mystery (#1)

Between volunteering for the annual pumpkin festival and coaching her girls to the state soccer finals, high school teacher Tj Jensen finds her good friend Zachary Collins dead in his favorite chair.

When the handsome new deputy closes the case without so much as a "why" or "how," Tj turns her attention from chili cook-offs and pumpkin carving to complex puzzles, prophetic riddles, and a decades-old secret she seems destined to unravel.

FATAL BRUSHSTROKE

Sybil Johnson

An Aurora Anderson Mystery (#1)

A dead body in her garden and a homicide detective on her doorstep...Computer programmer and tole-painting enthusiast Aurora (Rory) Anderson doesn't envision finding either when she steps outside to investigate the frenzied yipping coming from her own back yard. After all, she lives in a quiet California beach community where violent crime is rare and murder even rarer.

Suspicion falls on Rory when the body buried in her flowerbed turns out to be someone she knows—her tole-painting teacher, Hester Bouquet. Just two weeks before, Rory attended one of Hester's weekend seminars, an unpleasant experience she vowed never to repeat. As evidence piles up against Rory, she embarks on a quest to identify the killer and clear her name. Can Rory unearth the truth before she encounters her own brush with death?

CPSIA information can be obtained
at www.ICGtesting.com
Printed in the USA
LVHW081920150520
655691LV00011B/99/J